Angus

A Story about Finding Home

By Mark Leon Reeves

I would like to dedicate this book to my wife, Andrea, and my son, Brett. Without their love and support, I would have never been inspired to finish my first book!

Table of Contents

Chapter 1

*I*t's funny how your life can drastically change in a single day. When I woke up on Saturday, September 7, 2013, I had no idea how true the previous statement was. The memories from that day are permanently etched in my mind. It was my thirteenth birthday.

I awoke to the mouth-watering aroma of fried bacon and freshly brewed coffee. I took a quick peek out my window through the drawn mini-blinds. There wasn't a cloud in the sky. I glanced at the large thermometer hanging on the tree outside my window. It read seventy degrees. I looked at the large oak tree in the middle of our backyard. I could see the leaves moving in the wind slightly. *It doesn't get more perfect than that,* I thought as I got out of bed, and walked down the short hallway to our kitchen.

My German Shepard, MacGyver, was lying in the center of the living room chewing on a pig ear. He looked at me, wagged his tail, and went back to the pig ear.

My dad had given me MacGyver when he was only twelve weeks old for my tenth birthday. MacGyver slept next to my bed every night. He had obviously departed from my bedside for a fresh new pig ear from my dad.

As I entered the kitchen, I saw my dad. I stopped and watched him for a few seconds. He was wearing gray sweatpants and a solid black t-shirt. He was standing over an electric griddle pouring pancake batter onto the griddle. The griddle sizzled as the batter poured onto it.

Dad looked up and saw me standing there watching. "Good morning birthday boy!" Dad exclaimed.

"Morning Dad," I sleepily replied.

Dad turned back to his griddle and began placing strips of crispy bacon on top of the wet pancake batter on the griddle. My dad's famous bacon stuffed pancakes were my favorite!

I walked over to the coffee pot and poured me a large mug of coffee. I had been drinking coffee since I was nine years-old.

Dad flipped the pancakes and I heard the sizzle as the wet batter splattered against the hot griddle again.

"I have an extra special surprise for you today," Dad said as I poured a large amount of liquid French vanilla creamer from the fridge into my coffee.

The rich smell of the coffee helped awaken me more. The cold creamer cooled the coffee just enough for me to be able to take a large sip.

"I've been waiting a long time to show you this surprise," Dad said with a hint of excitement in his voice.

"Show me a surprise?" I asked curiously.

"Yes, it's not something I bought for you…it's something I am going to show you," Dad replied.

Dad handed me a large plate with two large pancakes with three strips of bacon in the center of each one. I sat the plate down on the kitchen counter, began spreading a thin layer of peanut butter on each pancake, and then poured maple syrup over the top.

"You will want to wear your field boots today. My surprise will be a little bit of a walk through a little bit of tough terrain," Dad said.

"Um… ok. When are we going?" I asked even more interested.

"As soon as you finish those pancakes. If you can finish them!" Dad replied with a smile and a wink.

Even though I was anxious to get going to find out what my surprise was, I sat down and savored every bit of my bacon- filled pancakes with peanut butter and maple syrup. I could probably eat bacon-filled pancakes every single day and never get tired of them!

After I finished my pancakes, I poured me another large mug of coffee for the road. I ran to my room and changed into my favorite pair of camouflaged cargo shorts, my Metallica t-shirt that I got when my dad took me to a live Metallica concert, and my khaki colored field boots.

When I returned to the kitchen, I laughed as I saw my dad was dressed almost identically to me.

"Great minds think alike!" Dad exclaimed.

Dad was also carrying a backpack. "What's the backpack for?" I asked.

"Well, we are going to be hiking for some ways. When we get to the surprise, we will probably be ready for some lunch," Dad answered.

"That's a big backpack for just lunch," I replied.

"Well, there are a few other items that I've been meaning to take, so I figured I'd take them today while I was thinking about it," Dad said.

This peaked my curiosity, but I knew it was of no use to ask dad to explain further. My dad was notorious for his surprises. He would never budge and give any hints or anything. He loved his surprises. I always looked forward to them.

Dad, MacGyver, and I walked out the front door into the glorious sunshine. The rising sun was just enough to provide warmth, but a slight breeze gently cooled the air.

We climbed in to Dad's 1974 Ford Bronco. My dad loved his Bronco. It was midnight blue with a white top. My dad and I had restored it when I was ten. We had spent countless hours together in the garage working on it while listening to Dad's favorite bands from the eighties- Metallica, Motley Crue, Poison, Skid Row, etc.

As we drove, I looked at my dad and thought about how lucky I was. My dad was the greatest man in the world. My mom died when I was only three. I don't really remember her. However, my dad told me that she was the most amazing woman he had ever known and that she loved me more than I could ever comprehend.

I have seen videos of my mom. But, I don't watch them anymore. I always got sad when I watched them. My dad said that's ok. He said I might want to watch them more when I get a little older.

My dad had never gotten involved with another woman after my mom died. I asked him one time why. He stated, "If I ever got involved with another woman, it would take away from the time I had to spend with you, Angus."

My dad and I were close. Very close!

Dad drove for about fifteen minutes on a country road that I had never been on before. MacGyver sat in the back seat with his head out the window enjoying the cool fifty-five miles per hour breeze.

Dad finally turned onto a gravel road. We drove down the gravel road for about five minutes and then Dad turned into a field and kept driving.

As the Bronco bounced up and down through the field, I thought it was strange for Dad to be driving through a field and I was extremely curious, but I sat quietly. I knew it wouldn't do me any good to ask any questions.

I looked at Dad. He had a sly smile on his face. I knew that he was fully aware that I was dying with curiosity and he loved every minute of it!

We came to the end of the field to what appeared to be a large forest. The field simply ended and then there was nothing but trees.

Dad finally broke his silence. "This is our land. I grew up in a house that use to stand in that field that we just drove across."

"What happened to the house?" I asked.

"The house burned down in 1989 when I was seventeen years old. Your grandma and grandpa decided that all of this land was too much to keep up with, so they moved to town. They never sold this land, and left it to me in their will," dad replied.

"So, you're leaving this land to me...that's my surprise?" I guessed.

"Well, you will eventually inherit this land. But, that's not your surprise," Dad said with a grin.

"I told you, you are going to have to walk for a while to get to your surprise. Have you done any walking yet?" Dad asked.

I simply shook my head.

"Ok then, let's get moving," Dad said as he patted me on the back, jumped out of the Bronco, and started off towards the woods.

MacGyver and I quickly jumped out and followed.

We walked for about forty-five minutes. I'm not sure how far we went, but Dad was right. The terrain was a little rough. We waded through creeks, climbed up steep hills, and walked through what looked like possibly snake-infested areas. I was grateful that I had listened to Dad and wore my field boots!

The whole time we were walking, Dad was telling me how he used to explore these woods when he was my age. He told me about his beagle, Spud, who he used to bring to these woods to hunt rabbits and squirrels.

We came to one part of the woods where a tiny log cabin stood. It wasn't really a log cabin. It looked more like a log outhouse. Dad said that he and his brother, Jeff, had spent days cutting down small trees and getting mud from the nearby creek to build this "clubhouse". It didn't have a door, but simply an opening to enter into it.

I peeked into the clubhouse and saw two round blocks of wood sitting inside. I thought to myself, *I spend hours playing Xbox every day. My dad spent his childhood exploring the forest, building clubhouses, and hunting with his dog!*

After looking at the clubhouse for a few minutes, Dad began walking again.

"How much further?" I asked.

"We're almost there," Dad said.

MacGyver seemed to sense what Dad said and seemed to get a little more excited.

As we approached a small creek, Dad stopped. He turned to me and said, "Look around and tell me what you see."

"I see a small creek with a large hill behind it," I said.

"Look really good, Angus! What else do you see?" Dad asked.

"OK, I also see a large boulder next to the creek by the hill," I stated quizzically.

I didn't understand my dad's inquiry.

"You're getting warmer, Angus! I walked past this area hundreds of times before I found it too...well, actually Spud found it!" Dad said with a laugh.

What in the world was dad talking about I wondered?

"Follow me!" exclaimed Dad.

We crossed the creek to where the boulder was. I saw etched in the boulder, "MM + EM". Dad saw me looking at the engraving.

"Mike McGuire plus Elizabeth Moore…your mom and I began dating when I was fifteen years old. I engraved that in 1987," Dad said with a smile that told me he was taking a trip down memory lane.

As I circled the boulder, I finally saw something that got me excited. Behind the boulder, in the hill there was an opening about two feet wide and two feet tall. A cave! It was perfectly hidden by the boulder and would only be found if you walked around the boulder. I still almost didn't see it, but I was really looking because I knew my dad had a surprise for me.

"A cave!" I almost yelled as I looked toward my dad.

My dad smiled and exclaimed, "Just wait until you see the inside of it!"

Dad opened the backpack and removed two flashlights. We had to get on our bellies and crawl into the cave. MacGyver refused to go in. He whined and simply sat down on his rear.

"It's ok Mac, you can wait outside if you want," Dad said.

After we crawled for about ten feet, the cave completely opened up and we were able to stand up. I shined my flashlight and saw that the cave was approximately thirty feet wide and thirty feet long.   I shined my light and saw that the ceiling of the cave was about fifteen feet high. I walked around the cave to look at every inch of it.

When I was ten, my dad and I went to Meramec Caverns in Stanton, Missouri. This cave was similar to that on a much smaller scale. There were no stalagmites or stalactites. However, there were several mineral formations. On the rear wall of the cave, I noticed a small opening. It was too small for me to get through. It was just a large crack really.

My dad noticed me looking at the opening and said, "The cave opens up through that crack".

I tried to shine my light through the opening, but I couldn't see into it.

"How do you know it opens up?" I asked.

"Yell into it," my dad said.

I pressed my mouth to the crack and yelled, "HELLO!"

"HELLO!" came back my echo.

Wow, that was cool. "How far back does it go?" I asked.

"I have no idea; I can't walk through walls!" laughed Dad.

As we stood in the cave my dad told me that the only people that he knew of that knew about this cave were him, my mom, and now me. Then he told me the news that really got me excited. He told me that he was selling our house in town, and building a new house on this land! This was the best surprise I could ever get!

Ever since I read *Where the Red Fern Grows* when I was in fourth grade, I wanted to live in the country. I ran over to my dad and gave him a hug. I don't know why I became so emotional, but I had to fight back the tears as I told my dad that I loved him and that this was definitely his best surprise ever!

"Oh, I almost forgot!" exclaimed dad as he opened the backpack and pulled out a slingshot, a roll of fishing line, a metal box containing 12 fishing hooks and sinkers, a magnesium fire starter, a Swiss Army knife, a roll of parachute cord, 2 ham sandwiches, a can of cheese Pringles, and 2 cans of Pepsi wrapped in aluminum foil.

"I know what the food and drink is for, but what's up with the other stuff?" I asked.

"Well, when I was about your age I had a wild idea that it would be neat to try to live off the land for a week with only these items. I took a week's vacation next week. I figured if you were up to the challenge, we'd spend next week right here with only these items!" Dad replied.

I didn't have to think about it but about 3 seconds. "That would be cool, Dad!" I exclaimed.

We spent about 20 minutes eating our lunch and talking about how we would try to use the slingshot to shoot game, the fishing line to catch fish, and the magnesium fire starter to build fires to cook our food and stay warm at night. The parachute cord could be used for a multitude of things. The uses of the knife were obvious. The more we talked, the more excited I got.

"There's a river about ten minutes north from here. We shouldn't have a problem catching our dinner there every night," Dad said with a big grin.

My dad had outdone himself when planning this adventure! "I'll just leave all of this stuff here in the cave. When we come out here next Saturday, we won't bring anything but the clothes on our backs!" Dad said excitedly.

"That sounds like a plan!" I said with a grin.

We crawled back out of the cave. MacGyver was lying beside the entrance patiently waiting for us. I gave him a pat on the head. We began our long trek back to the Bronco. I definitely had an extra spring in my step as the excitement about the upcoming week continued to build. Dad and I both shared our ideas of the kinds of things we would do to survive off the land for a whole week. Looking back, I would say that this was probably my happiest moment in my entire life!

It seemed like only a few minutes had passed when we came out of the thickness of the trees and into the open field where dad's Bronco sat. Dad, MacGyver, and I jumped in and we headed home.

As we drove, I couldn't think of anything else except our upcoming adventure in the woods. I suppose most kids wouldn't think of this as a fun time. However, I was different. The thought of the challenge of having to survive on our own with only the few supplies was awesome.

I knew the upcoming week was going to drag as I continued to count down the minutes until we left for our adventure. Dad put in his Metallica Ride the Lightening CD. The song Fade to Black blared from dad's speakers. MacGyver was once again enjoying the wind in his face out the window. I was looking out my window at a field of baled hay. I was thinking about the story my dad told me of how when he was a kid he and his friend, Scott, use to run across the field on the top of the large round bales. I never saw the log truck. All I remember was a sudden jolt and then complete darkness.

Chapter 2

I opened my eyes. At first, all I could see was bright white light. I squinted my eyes, the brightness from the light began to dim, and I could make out the room. I saw the I.V. stand with the I.V. bag attached beside my bed. I followed the clear plastic tubes from the bag down to my right arm.   I saw the monitor that kept track of my pulse and blood pressure. My left leg was elevated in some type of harness contraption about three feet off the bed. I was wearing only my underwear and a thin hospital gown. I saw a small 19-inch TV mounted in the corner of the room. My bed was the only one in the room. To my left was another door. I assumed it was a bathroom. There was an empty chair next to my bed. I was alone.

My last memory was looking out the window of my dad's Bronco watching bales of hay go by. Then, I remembered the sudden jolt. What had happened? I looked around the bed and saw a button. I figured this must be the call button, so, I pushed it.

Within twenty seconds, a young nurse with short auburn hair came briskly walking through the door.

"Oh my goodness! You're awake!" she exclaimed in awe.

"Where am I and what happened to me?" I asked.

"You are at Missouri Baptist Hospital, sweetie. You were in a very bad car wreck. My name is Amber. You have been in a coma for the past three weeks. We didn't know if you would wake up."

At first, what Amber said didn't register. I was in a car wreck? The last thing I remembered was looking out the window of my dad's Bronco at the large bales of hay in the field. Then it hit me. If I was in a coma, how was my dad?

I looked at Amber and asked, "How's my dad? Is he in a coma too?"

The look on Amber's face told me the answer before she spoke a word.

"Honey, there's no easy way to tell you this. Your dad didn't make it. Your dad's side of the vehicle was struck directly by a logging truck. I'm so sorry."

Amber stared at me as I lay in silence trying to comprehend the words she had just spoken. There had to be some mistake. Perhaps I was dreaming.

Amber continued, "Your uncle, Jeff, has been here to check on you a few times over the past three weeks. I'm going to call him and let him know you are awake. Is there anything I can do for you before I leave?"

"Did my dog die, too?" I asked.

Amber's response was a simple nodding of her head as she turned and left the room.

As soon as the door closed behind Amber, I was overwhelmed with a rush of the most intense sadness I had ever felt. I began weeping uncontrollably. How could this be true? My dad and I had just had the most amazing day ever! We were planning the most incredible week together imaginable. Now he was dead!

My sadness suddenly turned to rage! I ripped the I.V. out of my arm, grabbed my pillow from under my head and threw it as hard as I could across the room and screamed, "WHY? GOD, WHY DID YOU TAKE MY DAD FROM ME?"

I tried to pull my leg from the harness, but as I did, an intense pain shot up my leg. Amber came running through the door.

"Angus! Calm down! Lie back down. Your leg is broken and you have a brain injury. You could go back into a coma!" Amber screamed.

"I don't care! My dad is dead! My dog is dead! I might as well be dead!" I yelled.

Amber came to my bed and embraced me in a tight bear hug.

"I shouldn't have left you, Angus. I cannot imagine how you are feeling right now," Amber said softly against my ear as she hugged me tight.

I began to quiver as I sobbed. My body went limp as I continued to sob. Amber continued to hug me.

"God will get you through this storm, sweetheart. I'm here for you as well," Amber whispered into my ear.

I didn't know what to say. I just continued to cry. Amber sat holding me for several minutes without speaking another word as I cried.

Amber finally spoke again. "Your uncle, Jeff, is on his way to see you."

I had only seen my uncle a few times in my life. My dad wasn't close to his brother. My dad had told me that he and his brother were close growing up. But, something had changed Jeff. My dad wasn't sure what happened. He just said that Jeff changed and that they had grown apart.

I didn't know what to expect. But, I was glad somebody was coming to see me. Right now, all I had was Amber. I felt Amber's embrace let go and I looked into her eyes.

"Thank you," I said.

"You're welcome, Angus. I'm your friend now. I'm here for you anytime you need me!" Amber said.

At that moment, my uncle, Jeff, walked through the door.

"Angus! You really are awake!" Uncle Jeff said loudly as he walked through the door and came to my bedside.

Uncle Jeff looked at Amber, winked, and said, "Hello, sweet thing!"

Amber gave Uncle Jeff a disgusted look.

"I just told Angus about his Dad. He is in a very vulnerable place right now." Amber told Uncle Jeff in a stern voice.

Uncle Jeff replied, "Don't you worry your pretty little head. I'll take good care of Angus."

Uncle Jeff looked at me and said, "Angus, as soon as possible, you are coming to live with me."

I didn't know how to feel about this statement from my uncle. I was never close to him and he and my dad had not been on good terms. How would it be living with Uncle Jeff?

I stayed in the hospital for an additional nine days after I awoke from my coma. Amber and I became best friends. Amber worked Tuesday through Saturday from noon until nine. I know she had other patients, but I was convinced that I was her favorite. Every day she made numerous visits to my room. When she was not busy, she would sit beside me and we would talk. Mostly we talked about my dad.

At first, I would get upset trying to talk about him. However, the more we talked, the more I would smile when I remembered all of the good times my dad and I had. I told Amber about our plans to spend a week living off the land and staying in the hidden cave. I even described to her how to get to the cave.

I found out that Amber was only twenty-two years old. She had graduated from high school when she was seventeen and went straight to college and earned her bachelors of science in nursing in four years.

Not only was Amber beautiful, she was such a kind and caring person. She was very easy to talk to. It was as if I had known her my whole life. I didn't get nervous around her like I use to get around pretty girls at my school. For some reason, Amber genuinely cared about me. I found myself watching the clock. I couldn't wait for noon to roll around and I hated when nine o'clock came. The other nurses and doctors were all nice, but Amber was special! I didn't understand at the time, but there was something about Amber that instantly bonded us.

Uncle Jeff only visited me one other day during those nine days after my awakening. He said he was too busy at work and the fact that he lived an hour and a half from the hospital made it impossible for him to come any other days. I didn't mind. I felt uncomfortable around my uncle.

I was still mourning the loss of my hero, my dad. I think I would have lost my mind if it weren't for Amber. Amber gave me her cell phone number and told me to call or text her any time after I got out of the hospital if I needed a friend to talk to. I told her I would.

I was released from the hospital on Monday, October 7, 2013. I was not excited to leave. First, I was not going home. I was going to Uncle Jeff's house. Uncle Jeff told me that he had already gotten all of my belongings from my old house and that there was no need for me to go back there. Second, Amber was off on Monday. I was not even going to get to say goodbye.

Uncle Jeff was helping me get into my wheelchair when she walked through the door. She was wearing a yellow sundress with blue flowers on it and brown cowboy boots. This was the first time I had seen Amber not wearing her nursing attire. She was radiant! She walked over and gave me a big tight hug. I could smell the apple scented shampoo in her hair.

"You came in on your day off to tell me goodbye!" I said in a choked up voice as we hugged.

"Did you think I would let my best friend leave without a proper goodbye?" Amber asked not letting go.

Amber finally let go and looked at me with a big smile. I noticed a tear streaming down her cheek.

"You are an amazing young man, Angus! I am blessed beyond measure to have had the past nine days to get to know you. I really hope you'll keep in touch!" Amber said holding back her emotions.

"Without you, I think I would have lost my mind. From the bottom of my heart, thank you for being my friend!" I responded.

Uncle Jeff stepped in between us and declared, "Ok, enough of that mush! We need to get on the road. I want to make it home in time to watch Monday Night Football!"

Again, I could see the displeasure on Amber's face.

"I meant what I said. I will always be there for you if you need me," Amber stated, turned, and walked out of the room.

I watched her as she walked out the door and wondered if I would ever see her again. I noticed Uncle Jeff watching her as she walked away also.

Uncle Jeff pushed me in my wheel chair to the elevators. We rode down the elevators in an uncomfortable silence. We came out of the elevators into a long corridor that led to a parking garage. Uncle Jeff pushed me to another set of elevators and we rode that elevator, again in silence, to the blue level of the parking garage. We exited that elevator and Uncle Jeff pushed me to a silver Ford F-150 Lariat.

"Don't think I'm going to be helping you get out of that wheelchair! You are going to have to learn how to get around on you own. Now's as good a time as any to start!" Uncle Jeff said in a gruff voice.

I noticed an immediate change for the worse in Uncle Jeff's demeanor now that he was not around other people. Using the wheel chairs arm rests, I pushed myself up to a standing position on one leg. I opened the truck's door and bent down with my one good leg. I was still weak. I used my one good arm to pull myself up into the truck and plopped down into the truck. I saw a pair of crutches in the back seat of the truck.

Uncle Jeff sighed in disgust and exclaimed, "You've got a long way to go princess!"

Chapter 3

We pulled up to Uncle Jeff's house at dusk. Uncle Jeff's house was nothing like I expected. It was actually very nice. It was an artisan style house with tan siding and beautiful rock pillars on the porch.

The yard and landscaping were meticulous. There was a large flagpole in the center of the yard. A bright floodlight illuminated the large American flag at the top of the pole.

Uncle Jeff hopped out of the truck without paying much attention to me and walked into the house. I slid carefully out of the truck, hopped to the back door of the truck, and got my crutches from the back seat.

I had never used crutches before and I wasn't very good with them. I managed to make it across the driveway, but when I got to the steps on the front porch, I had a little trouble. I stepped up on the first step and pulled the crutches up to the step. I braced myself on the crutches and attempted to step up to the second step. When I did, I felt weak, lost my balance, fell up, and landed awkwardly on the porch with a loud thud. My broken leg let me know it was still not completely healed. I winced in pain, but tried not to make any further noise. I didn't want Uncle Jeff to come back out and belittle me.

I managed to stand back up, picked up my crutches, and walked into Uncle Jeff's house.

As I entered the house, I saw Uncle Jeff sitting on a brown leather couch with a bottle of beer in his hand watching football on the biggest flat screen TV I'd ever seen.

The room appeared spotless. The flooring was a gunstock oak with a large burgundy area rug underneath a colonial style coffee table in front of the couch. It was so clean that it appeared to be brand new.   There were two burgundy wingback chairs at opposite ends of the couch that matched the rug.

Without looking away from the game, Uncle Jeff said, "Your room is down in the basement. It's the last room on the left."

So, the guy with the broken leg and the brain injury gets a room down stairs in the basement! Either Uncle Jeff didn't consider these facts, or he did it just to be a jerk. Probably the latter! I already knew better than to point these facts out to my uncle.   I simply replied, "Ok, thanks."

The stairway to the basement was between the living room and the kitchen. I had better luck going down the basement stairs than I did going up the porch steps. It took me a while, but I managed to make it without falling.

The basement wasn't nearly as nice as the main floor, but it was definitely clean. The floors were bare concrete. The walls were unfinished drywall. The lights were the kind with the light sockets with the pull strings.

The first room I walked past was on my right. I saw a washer and dryer and several laundry baskets stacked neatly beside them inside.

The next room was on my left. This room was a bathroom. It contained a toilet, a pedestal sink, and a small corner shower.

I passed two more rooms with the doors closed to them and finally made it to my room. Half of the room contained large *Rubbermaid* tubs stacked three high. There was a handmade shelving unit against the wall to my left. Three shelves ran all the way across the wall. The shelves had numerous boxes stacked neatly on them of unknown content. The remaining part of the room was a small section about six feet wide and six feet long. An old army cot with a single pillow and a brown blanket sat in this section. The cot only stood about a foot above the ground, which made it extremely difficult for me to bend down to lay down. I managed to lie down.

I didn't sleep much that first night in Uncle Jeff's house. My mind would not shut off. I thought about my last day with Dad and cried a lot. I thought about my new friend, Amber. This brought a smile to my face. I thought about my dog, MacGyver. This made me cry again. I thought about how drastically my life had changed in the proverbial blink of an eye. What was it going to be like living with Uncle Jeff? I already knew the answer to this question... MISERABLE! I finally fell asleep around 3 a.m.

• • •

"Rise and shine Princess!" Uncle Jeff said in a booming voice.

I was immediately awake and my heart was pounding rapidly from the adrenaline from being awakened in such a startling manner.

I quickly opened my eyes to see Uncle Jeff standing over me. I have no idea why, but his body language told me that he was angry.

"What time is it?" I asked.

"It's time to get up, that's what time it is!" Uncle Jeff exclaimed as he turned around and walked out of the room.

"Be upstairs in two minutes!" He added as he was walking out.

I got up from the cot as quickly as I could, grabbed my crutches, and headed upstairs.

Upon arriving upstairs, I saw Uncle Jeff sitting at the kitchen table eating a bowl of cereal and drinking a beer. The clock on the microwave told me it was 5:30 a.m.!

"If you want any breakfast, you better sit down and eat. I have to leave in 15 minutes," Uncle Jeff said.

Why was he angry? Was he mad at me about something?

"Where are you going and why are you leaving so early?" I asked.

"I have to go to work and you have to get ready for school sweetheart," Uncle Jeff replied sarcastically.

Uncle Jeff owned his own construction company. He was wearing Carhart jeans, a blue t-shirt, and brown work boots.

"School doesn't start until eight," I replied.

"Well, if I don't make sure you're up before I leave for work, you'll probably just go back to bed and skip school. Your bus will be here to pick you up at 7:20. You will eat breakfast and take a shower before I leave. Make sure you wipe the shower down when you're done. I don't want a dirty shower! Capeesh?" Uncle Jeff exclaimed.

I didn't dare argue or try to explain to Uncle Jeff that I had never been late or skipped school a day in my life.

"Yes, sir," I replied fearfully.

I poured a small bowl of cereal and went to the fridge to get the milk. Once at the fridge I realized that it was going to be very difficult to carry the bowl of cereal with milk while using my crutches. I started to ask Uncle Jeff for help, but then realized that that was probably a bad idea.

I returned to the table, sat down, and began eating my cereal without any milk. Uncle Jeff looked at me, made a sarcastic snicker, and simply shook his head in disgust.

After eating my dry cereal, I hobbled back down to the basement and took a shower. With extra care, I wiped the inside of the shower dry when I was done.

I went to my room and began looking through the *Rubbermaid* containers for my clothes. Of course, it was the last container that I opened that contained my clothes. I put on a pair of jeans, my favorite Dallas Cowboy sweatshirt, and my black Converse All-Star sneakers.

I went back upstairs and sat down on the couch. Uncle Jeff was walking out the door to go to work. As he was walking out he said, "Have a nice day at school, Precious!" The door slammed loudly behind him. I heard the roar of his truck pull out of the driveway.

I made my way over to one of the wingback chairs and sat down. For the first time I thought about my friend, Anthony. Anthony had been my best friend since first grade. Anthony was my only friend at school. All of the other kids made fun of my speech impediment and acted as if I had leprosy or something.

I had no idea what I was going to do, but I knew after one night with my uncle, that I couldn't continue living with him. I didn't have my plan yet. It was at this moment that I came to a decision. I would not stay at my uncle's house very long!

Chapter 4

*D*o you know what the funny thing is about the old cliché about walking on egg shells is? It is impossible! You cannot walk on eggshells without them breaking! So, why even try?

I carefully boarded the bus at 7:20 a.m. sharp. I knew from the previous night that going up steps was more challenging than going down. I didn't want to fall up the steps getting on the bus. The other kids on the bus didn't pay any attention to me. My school was a small school. Surely, the whole school had heard about me and my dad's horrendous wreck. Surely, they had heard that my dad had died. I couldn't tell from the kids on the bus reaction to me boarding.

I sat down in a seat at the front of the bus and watched as we pulled away from Uncle Jeff's house. Anybody who saw this house would think that a very nice family lived there. It's funny how people judge other people based on things like the type of cars they drive or by how nice the house is that they live in.

• • •

When I arrived at school, Anthony was waiting outside for me. Anthony was a quirky kid. He was pretty much an outcast just like me. He was sporting his trademark fedora that he had been wearing since he was in fifth grade along with black jeans and a black Misfits t-shirt.

The other kids had made fun of Anthony when he started wearing the hat, but Anthony didn't seem to mind. He liked the hat and kept wearing it. Eventually the other kids realized that Anthony was unfazed by their remarks and left him alone.

Anthony ran up to me and gave me a big hug. "Dude, I am so sorry about your dad!"

Anthony said as he hugged me almost causing me to fall.

"Thanks buddy," I replied.

"Where are you living? Are you in foster care?" Anthony asked.

"No, I'm living with my uncle," I said woefully.

"That's a bad thing?" Anthony asked.

Anthony could read me like a book.

"My uncle is a jerk! I've never met someone so mean!" I said emphatically.

"Oh man, that sucks! Maybe your uncle is just upset. I mean, your dad was his brother," Anthony said.

"No man, my uncle and my dad were not close. I don't know what it is, but I think my uncle is mad at me! I haven't done anything but be nice and respectful and he hates me!" I responded.

I immediately regretted my outburst and I knew Anthony wouldn't understand so I quickly changed the subject.

"If it's ok with my uncle, do you think I could crash at your place tonight?" I asked.

"Of course bro, my mom is fixing her famous lasagna for dinner. She would love to see you! Call me if your uncle says its ok, and I'm sure my mom will come pick you up," Anthony said enthusiastically.

"I will. We had better get to class. It might take me a while to get there!" I said trying to sound upbeat.

"I'll carry your stuff for you buddy," Anthony offered.

"Thanks man," I said as we headed to our first hour class.

I couldn't focus on my schoolwork very much that day. Seventh hour was my study hall time. I checked out a new book to read with the hopes it would take my mind off everything.

I loved to read. Reading had been my escape since I was very young. I chose the book *My Side of the Mountain*. It was about a young boy named Sam Gribley who decided to run away from home and live on his own in the Catskill Mountains.

Looking back, I am convinced that I was led to that book. If it hadn't been for that book, I probably wouldn't have chosen the path that I did. I spent my whole study hall reading. The more I read, the more I began thinking about my plan.

Eighth hour was social studies. The class had been studying the Revolutionary war while I was in the hospital and was taking a test over the unit. My teacher, Mr. Mills, said that I could read while the class took the test and I could start back up fresh on the next unit. "*Perfect*" I thought. I spent all of 8th hour reading as well. By the end of 8th hour, I was already halfway through my book.

After school, I rode the bus to Uncle Jeff's house. I read the entire time I was on the bus. I never could call Uncle Jeff's house "home".

Uncle Jeff wasn't home yet. As I entered the house, the house had a feeling of doom about it. I don't know what it was, but even the house seemed to hate me!

I made it down to my room in the basement, laid down on my cot, and continued reading my book. The house was completely quiet. I had escaped from all of my worries and was now in the Catskill Mountains with Sam Gribley!

Around five o'clock I heard the door upstairs slam. "ANGUS! GET YOUR ASS UP HERE!" Uncle Jeff screamed.

I had been so entranced in my book that I hadn't heard Uncle Jeff's truck pull up nor him open the door. My heart immediately began pounding rapidly. Uncle Jeff was very angry. *What did I do?* I made it upstairs as quickly as I could.

Uncle Jeff was standing in the doorway holding a leaf. His face was red. I could see his pulse beating in the side of his neck.

"WHAT THE HELL IS THIS?" Uncle Jeff yelled furiously.

"A leaf...," I stated nervously.

"I know it's a damn leaf! Why is it in the house?" Uncle Jeff said angrily.

"Um, I don't know," I said.

"Well, you're the only one who has been in my house!" Uncle Jeff roared.

"I'm sorry, Uncle Jeff. It must have stuck to one of my crutches when I was walking in," I said.

"Oh, it got stuck to one of your crutches! Well, don't you think you could have looked at your crutches when you came in?" Uncle Jeff stated in a mocking manner.

I couldn't believe my uncle was this angry over single leaf. Nevertheless, I didn't dare point this out.

"I'm sorry, it won't happen again," I said timidly.

"You're damn right it won't happen again! You know why it won't happen again? Because you're going to spend your evening raking all of the leaves in the yard! There's a rake in the garage!" Uncle Jeff said furiously.

I couldn't believe what I was hearing. I had a broken leg and was recovering from a brain injury. Because I had accidently brought a single leaf into the house I was going to spend all evening raking leaves while on crutches!

"Yes sir," was my simple response as I headed to the garage to retrieve the rake.

I forgot all about my plans with Anthony. I spent two and a half hours raking Uncle Jeff's yard that evening. Uncle Jeff would periodically walk outside to inspect my work.

The yard wasn't big. I was afraid of what would happen if I missed a single leaf. I took great care to insure there wasn't a single leaf left in the yard! It was very difficult raking while balancing myself on my crutches at the same time!

Although I didn't think about Anthony, I did spend the two and a half hours thinking about how I was going to escape from Uncle Jeff's house. I thought about the character, Sam Gribley, in my book. Sam had simply run away from home. Surprisingly, his parents didn't seem to mind. I knew my case was not this simple. I had only been living with my uncle for a couple of days. I already knew that my uncle was a very controlling man. I was scared of my uncle! If I simply ran away, he would hunt me down, find me, and punish me. I had to have a plan. Simply running away would not work!

Chapter 5

*T*he next day at school I apologized to Anthony about not calling him. I told him about the leaf and how I had spent all evening raking leaves.

"Are you freaking serious? Your uncle has some serious issues!" Anthony said.

"I know right!" I said.

"Tonight's meatloaf night. It's not lasagna, but you're welcome to come over if you want," Anthony said quickly changing the subject.

"I'll try. But I can't make any promises," I said.

"Just don't drag any leaves into the house. As a matter a fact, maybe you should go home and clean the house before your uncle gets home," Anthony suggested.

"That's a good idea! It's worth a try. I need to get out of that house!" I replied.

Anthony and I walked to class together. I spent every free minute reading my book. I finished it during my free time in my sixth hour English class.

After school, I walked straight into Uncle Jeff's house and began cleaning. I swept the hardwood floors, dusted all of the furniture, and cleaned all of the windows. I would have done more, but just as I was finishing the windows, I saw Uncle Jeff pull into the driveway.

I took a quick look around the house. I couldn't see a speck of dust anywhere. The windows were completely transparent.

Uncle Jeff walked through the door.

"Good evening, Uncle Jeff," I said, trying to sound pleasant.

"What's so good about it?" Uncle Jeff asked gruffly.

I was already getting use to my uncle's irritability.

"I swept the floors, dusted all of the furniture, and cleaned all of the windows for you," I said trying to stay upbeat.

"You did all of that for me?" Uncle Jeff questioned.

Something about his tone of voice told me that my hopes of pleasing my uncle were going to be in vain.

"Yes, sir. I know how much you like to keep your house clean. So, I thought I'd help you out by cleaning the house," I said nervously.

"You thought you'd help ME out, did you?" Uncle Jeff asked.

"Yes sir," I said wondering where my uncle was going with his questions.

Raising his voice, Uncle Jeff asked, "Who lives in this house, darling?"

"Ummmm," I stammered.

"UMMMM IS NOT AN ANSWER!" Uncle Jeff yelled.

Uncle Jeff continued, "YOU and I both live in this house. So, don't think you were helping ME out by cleaning. Do you think I'm here to cook and clean and take care of you?"

"N-N-N-NO sir I was just trying to do something nice for you. I was hoping to make you happy," I stuttered.

"Oh, were you now? I suppose there's nothing in it for you either?" Uncle Jeff questioned as he glared at me with a hate in his eyes that I couldn't understand.

"N-N-N-O sir," I stuttered again.

"Well, in that case, thank you from the bottom of my heart for your grand gesture of kindness!" Uncle Jeff exclaimed as he bowed in sarcasm, walked to the kitchen, and got a beer out of the fridge. I made a quick exit to my room in the basement to avoid any further confrontation.

I knew that my plan of asking to go to Anthony's had failed. There was no way I was going to ask to go to Anthony's house after my uncle's unexplainable fit of rage over me cleaning the house.

Perhaps I should have anticipated my uncle's reaction. I had not. I was in complete shock over my uncle's rage over me busting my butt trying to please him.

I was initially very scared of my uncle. However, my fear turned into anger. Of course, I didn't dare get cross with him. He was much bigger than I was and I knew he would hurt me if I revealed my anger.

I didn't go back upstairs for dinner. I couldn't stand the thought of being around my uncle again. I wished I had gotten another book to read to get my mind off things. Instead, I lay on my cot thinking more about the character in the book I had just finished. My mind wondered for several hours before I finally fell asleep for the night.

• • •

I was awakened at one in the morning. I heard a woman's voice coming from upstairs. I couldn't help myself; I had to go see who was in the house.

I slowly snuck up the stairs and peered into the living room. A pretty blond girl, probably in her late twenties, was sitting on the couch beside Uncle Jeff. She was giggling and nibbling on Uncle Jeff's ear. I noticed a white powder spread out into three thin straight lines on the coffee table in front of Uncle Jeff and the girl. There was also a small straw beside the powder. I didn't understand what was going on at the time. I had no idea what the white stuff on the coffee table was.

The sight of the pretty girl nibbling on my uncle's ear disgusted me. I sat crouched at the top of the stairs watching my uncle and the girl for several minutes. The more I watched the more appalled I became. I couldn't stand it. I turned around and quietly returned to the basement.

• • •

The next day at school was pretty much a repeat of the previous day. I told Anthony about my uncle's episode of anger. I didn't mention the late night scene I had witnessed. I was embarrassed about that.

Anthony was sympathetic, but he didn't really know what to say. He told me that if I could ever get out of my uncle's house that I could come over any time. I told him I appreciated the offer and that perhaps I could come over on the weekend.

During my seventh hour study hall, I managed to get a new book to read. This time I chose the book *Hatchet.*

I again went home after school and cleaned. This time, I swept the floor, cleaned the upstairs and basement bathroom, and did laundry. I had to keep Uncle Jeff happy until I figured out what to do.

Uncle Jeff came home an hour earlier than usual. Upon entering the house, I didn't dare say anything about the work I had done. I simply said, "Hello, Uncle Jeff."

"Hello, Angus. I forgot to tell you. I'm taking you to get your cast taken off. Let's go," Uncle Jeff replied in a civil tone.

We rode to the doctor's office listening to Hank Williams Jr. sing about all of his rowdy friends settling down. The doctor's office sat directly behind a Burger King. I could smell the food. It smelled amazing. I hadn't had a cheeseburger in a long time! This was the same Burger King that my dad used to bring me to when I was a little kid. I use to love playing in the play area! My dad would sit and drink coffee and let me play for as long as I liked.

Getting my cast removed was uneventful. The doctor came into the room and cut off the cast. The saw was very loud and vibrated. The vibration of the saw actually tickled when the doctor was cutting off the cast. The doctor made two cuts on the cast. One cut was made in the front and one was made in the back.

Next, the doctor used a tool that he informed me was called a cast spreader to open the cast up from the two cuts he made. After he spread the cast apart and removed the hard plaster, he used a pair of large scissors with blunt tips to cut away the padding that had been underneath the hard cast. That was it.

The doctor told Uncle Jeff that my leg had healed nicely and that after a few weeks I should be pretty much back to normal. He went on to say that, there was no need for physical therapy. That I should simply ease back into my regular routine.

Ease back into my regular routine? I wondered to myself if raking leaves for two and a half hours and doing housework for two to three hours every day was considered "easing" back into my normal routine!

We left the doctor's office. Uncle Jeff said he needed to run into Menards and pick up a few items. Menards is a local home improvement superstore.

"What do you have to get?" I asked simply to try to invoke a conversation.

"Don't worry about it!" Uncle Jeff snapped back.

"Ok, I'm sorry," I said.

Wow! I had thought Uncle Jeff was in a better mood today. I was obviously mistaken.

As we walked into Menards, I noticed a bulletin board in the entryway that caught my attention. On the bulletin board were pictures of missing children. There were tons of them!

As I looked at all of the posters, I thought about all of the loving parents whose lives were destroyed when their children disappeared.

One of the posters was for a girl named Gina Dawn Brooks. My father had told me about her. Gina Dawn Brooks was a thirteen-year old girl who had disappeared from a nearby town in 1989. My dad had vividly remembered this because that was the year he graduated from high school.

My dad had told me that Gina was abducted while riding her bike. The police found the bike, but had never found Gina. My dad had worked at a prison that was located about ten miles from our house. One of the inmates there was a suspect in the abduction of Gina. In an attempt to get his sentence reduced for other crimes, the inmate had told the police that he was the getaway driver during Gina's abduction. He provided details to where her body was supposedly buried. The police conducted a thorough search of the area where he said her body was, but they were unable to find any remains. To this day, Gina Dawn Brooks is still missing.

I followed Uncle Jeff around Menards without saying a word. Uncle Jeff bought several type of cleaning agents, some lightbulbs, trash bags, and five bags of water softener salt.

When we returned to the truck, Uncle Jeff told me to load up the 50-pound bags of salt into the truck. I did as I was told, and we headed home. For some reason, I thought about the Gina Dawn Brooks' poster the entire ride home.

When we got back to Uncle Jeff's house, I carried the water softener salt into the house and poured it into the water softener (which I found out was in the corner of the laundry room in the basement).

Next, I went to my room and laid down on my cot. I wasn't tired, but I closed my eyes and began thinking. The Gina Dawn Brooks poster was still in my thoughts. Why was I dwelling on this? A girl had simply vanished almost thirty years ago. I had known about this since my dad told me about it about five years ago. I hadn't really thought much about it when dad told me the story. I knew my dad told me this because he wanted me to be careful. Yet today I couldn't stop thinking about it.

I saw the picture of Gina on the poster in my mind. I visualized the police finding her bike. I wondered if there was a chance that Gina was still alive somewhere. That is when it hit me! I had seen movies where people faked their own death. However, I had never heard of any kid faking his own kidnapping.

I laid on my cot until 2 a.m. thinking about how I could fake my own kidnapping. When I started reading My Side of the Mountain, I had thought about simply running away. I knew that that was a bad idea. Uncle Jeff would hunt me down and find me. He would probably treat me even worse than he did now if I tried running away and was caught! Would he still keep searching for me if he thought someone kidnapped me? He might. He might not.

I figured if Uncle Jeff and the police thought I had been kidnapped, their search would be completely different. They wouldn't be trying to figure out where I went. They would be trying to figure out who took me and where someone else took me.

I knew I couldn't simply get on a train or bus and go somewhere. There would be people on the train or bus that would report seeing a thirteen-year-old boy all by himself. I had to go somewhere where no one would see me. I had to become invisible to society. MY DAD'S CAVE! That was the perfect place! How was I going to get all the way there without being seen? Wouldn't search dogs track my scent? I had to make a plan. I couldn't simply just take off. If I did, people would see me, and Uncle Jeff would find me. I decided that I couldn't rush into this. I had to make a plan and be smart!

Chapter 6

I was actually excited to go to school the next day. You might think that the thought of faking your own kidnapping and running away to survive off the land for the rest of your life would make a thirteen-year old kid nervous. I can honestly say that I was not nervous. For some reason, I felt at peace with my decision.

I thought about my dad showing me the cave. I thought about the book *My Side of the Mountain* that I read. I thought about how I had been drawn to the Gina Dawn Brooks poster. It was as if I was being directed to do this.

As I sat in each of my classes that day, I would jot down ideas of things I needed to research as they popped into my head. I knew I would have time during my seventh hour study hall to do my research. Like I said, I wanted to be smart. I had to plan this out perfectly. My escape needed to go off without a hitch. I honestly feared that if Uncle Jeff caught me, he would seriously hurt me...or worse!

I went straight to a computer in my seventh hour study hall. I had my list of things to look up. My list contained the following items to research:

1. *How to throw dogs off your scent?*
2. *Edible plants in Missouri*
3. *How to make water safe to drink?*
4. *Survival tips*

My first search, "How to throw dogs off of your scent", provided some very interesting results. First, I always assumed that dogs simply followed your body's odor. I discovered that this is not 100% accurate. According to my research, search dogs actually detect your scent from dead skin cells that are constantly falling off your body. So, if a person simply puts on clean clothes or someone else's clothes, a search dog will still be able to track you because you have dead skin cells that constantly fall off of your body. I had no idea of this. So, how does a person prevent dead skin cells from falling off their body? One particular website stated that in theory a person could coat their entire body with petroleum jelly. The petroleum jelly would provide a seal of the skin that would prevent any dead skin cells from falling off. This made sense! So, I added to my list- *Find a large jar of petroleum jelly!*

My second search, *edible plants in Missouri*, only provided three results. The three plants that came up in my search were morel mushrooms, Virginia waterleaf, and yellow wood sorrel. I made some notes and drew sketches of each of these. I expanded my search to *"edible berries in Missouri"*. Every website I found strongly cautioned eating berries unless you were sure that the berry was edible. The websites advised that if a person became sick from eating poisonous berries they would suffer severe stomach cramps, diarrhea, and dehydration. All of these would make it extremely difficult for the person to do the necessary tasks in order to survive in the wilderness. I decided to use the strategy utilized by Sam Gribley. I would watch the birds. If birds ate it, then it was safe for me to eat.

My third search, *"how to make water safe to drink"* provided me with all kinds of methods. There were numerous recommendations for water filtration devices. There was a method of adding a very small amount of bleach to your drinking water. I couldn't order a water filtration device. I knew I could never pack enough bleach to last me a lifetime.

Finally, I stumbled across a website that recommended simply using a stainless steel coffee mug to boil the water to purify it. This was simple enough! I could easily take a stainless steel coffee mug with me. As long as I took care of the mug and didn't allow it to stay wet, it wouldn't rust and should last me a lifetime! I just had to find one to take! I added to my list- *Find a large stainless steel coffee mug*.

My last search was by far the most productive. Try typing survival tips in any search engine. You will find a plethora of information! I came across a website that provided me with numerous types of herbal medicine that I could use in the wilderness if needed. I jotted down three pages of notes and sketches of the various types of plants that I might be able to find to make medicine from. I had not thought about needing medicine, but after seeing it on the website, I knew this information was of utmost importance!

I found another website that had a list of edible insects. I hadn't thought about eating bugs; but I knew that if necessary, I would do it! I'm not a real squeamish type of person.

I use to watch a show called *Fear Factor*. I would watch contestants on the show have to eat bugs in order to win a challenge. I remembered one episode were a woman had to eat some hissing cockroaches. She could not do it! Not even a single cockroach! I couldn't believe anybody couldn't force themselves to eat a few bugs. Hissing cockroaches are disgusting, but this woman had a chance to win $50,000! I had told my dad that I could eat a pound of hissing cockroaches for $50,000 dollars! My dad had laughed and said if he ever won a lot of money, he would pay to see that.

I also found a website on how to catch fish in a survival situation. I had thought that I would just simply use the equipment dad had left in the cave and go catch fish by attaching the fishing line to a stick. This website provided instructions on how to catch fish by attaching fishing line to tree branches (several of them so you could have numerous lines in the water at the same time!). When the fish took the bait and pulled it under water, the natural tension from the tree limbs would hook the fish. All you had to do was watch for the tree limbs to start bending down. Another genius idea!

The website also instructed on how to find natural bait, where to fish during the different seasons, and how weather conditions affected fishing. I was amazed and excited about all of the information I was able to find in such a short amount of time! By the time my 45-minute study hall was over, I had seventeen pages of notes and drawings!

I spent the next two days in study hall doing research on survival skills. By the time I was finished, I had forty-two pages of notes on various survival techniques and tips. The only thing I had left to do was to get a large jar of petroleum jelly and a stainless steel coffee mug. I didn't like the thought of stealing these items, even from my uncle. My dad had always stressed to me the importance of honesty. Nevertheless, I knew that if I was going to follow through with my plan, I had no other choice.

Chapter 7

On Friday, October 25th, I ran from the bus into Uncle Jeff's house. I knew that I should have a couple of hours to clean the house and try to locate a jar of petroleum jelly and a stainless steel coffee mug before Uncle Jeff got home from work.

I went into Uncle Jeff's upstairs bathroom and began looking for a jar of petroleum jelly. I was very careful and put everything back exactly as it was. If I moved an item, I was careful to set it back exactly as it was before I touched it. I didn't find any petroleum jelly in the upstairs bathroom.

I went downstairs to the basement.

I was scrounging through the basement getting desperate when the upstairs phone rang. The sound of the phone startled me and my heart immediately began pounding rapidly in my chest. The whole time I had been staying at my uncles, this was the first time I had heard the phone ring.

"Hello?" I answered the phone.

"Angus?" The voice on the other end of the phone inquired.

"Amber?" I replied suddenly overwhelmed with joy.

"Angus, honey! Why haven't you called? Are you doing ok?" Amber asked.

Her voice melted my heart. I had thought about her since I left the hospital, but I had failed to fulfill my promise and call her. I felt a tear stream down my cheek as my rapidly beating heart began to return to normal rhythm.

"I'm sorry, Amber. I've been really busy getting settled in at my uncle's house," I said.

"I figured you'd need some time to get settled. Your uncle gave me a funny vibe. Is he treating you ok?" Amber asked with genuine concern.

"He's not my dad, but I'm doing ok," I lied.

Amber seemed to sense my untruthfulness.

"Listen, Angus, I meant what I said. I am always here for you. If you need anything, please don't hesitate to ask and let me help you," Amber said emphatically.

"Thanks, Amber. I'm sorry if I worried you. After I am settled in here, maybe I could take you and show you my cave! I'll call again when I have more time. Thanks for calling me. Again, I'm sorry I didn't call," I said.

I didn't want to hang up the phone. Every fiber of my being wanted to continue talking to Amber. Her voice had such a comforting effect on me. But, I kept thinking, I *have to find the petroleum jelly and the steel mug before Uncle Jeff gets home!*

"Ok, Angus. I'd love to go see your cave! Just remember, I'm off on Sundays and Mondays. Please call me when you have more time to talk!" Amber replied enthusiastically.

"I will. Goodbye Amber," I answered and then hung up the phone.

At first, I was smiling from ear to ear. I was picturing Amber in her yellow sundress with the blue flowers and cowboy boots. I felt so lucky to have such a wonderful girl for a friend. Then, it struck me. If I followed through with my plan, I would never be able to see or talk to Amber again! What choice did I have? I couldn't continue living with my uncle!   I shook my head and let out a loud yell, "AAAAAAAGGGGGGHHHHHH!"

I went back to the basement and continued looking for the petroleum jelly. I had to steady myself. I was extremely angry at the situation and quickly realized that I was not being careful. I was not putting things back as they were. If Uncle Jeff noticed that I had been snooping through his house, my whole plan could be ruined. I took a deep breath and slowly let it out to calm myself.

I went to my room and noticed the cardboard boxes on the shelving unit against the wall. I walked over to the boxes. I noticed one of the boxes labeled "*First-Aid Supplies*". I opened the box and found rubbing alcohol, hydrogen peroxide, and bandages of various sizes, gauze, medical tape, antibacterial ointment, and a large jar of PETROLEUM JELLY!

"YES!" I said aloud.

Now I knew where the petroleum jelly was. I closed the box up and made sure it was setting on the shelf exactly as it was before so attention would not be drawn to it.

I saw a box labeled *"Halloween Costumes"*. I don't know why I opened it; I guess I was just curious. The box was packed full of various costumes- a police officer's uniform, an Indian, a zombie, and even a giant banana! There were also numerous wigs inside the box.

As I was looking through the costumes, a light bulb went off in my head. I was going to be walking for quite a way in order to reach my dad's cave. There was a very good chance that someone would see me walking. I needed a disguise! The wigs provided a perfect disguise! I found a black wig that was obviously used to go along with the 80's rocker costume that I also found in the box. The wig looked like Tommy Lee on the cover of *Motley Crue's Shout at the Devil* CD. I decided this wig was the perfect one. I didn't think anyone would describe seeing a thirteen- year old boy if I was wearing this!

Next, I found a box on the shelf labeled *"Camping Supplies"*. I opened the box and could not believe what I saw! If it had been a movie, there would have been a golden beam shining on it with angels singing *Hallelujah* as I opened the box!

In the center of the box was a large heavy-duty stainless steel camping mug. The mug was obviously an expensive item. The stainless steel was very thick. The mug was much heavier than I expected when I lifted it. The mug also had a very heavy duty handle on it. I couldn't believe it! I was so happy that I began crying. I said a quick prayer of thanks.

Then, I heard it. The front door slammed!

"ANGUS!" Uncle Jeff screamed from upstairs.

I had been so caught up in my thoughts about Amber and my search for the petroleum jelly and coffee mug that I had lost track of time. I hadn't done my daily cleaning of Uncle Jeff's house!

I quickly folded the lids back in on the box and placed the box back on the shelf. I took an extra couple of seconds to look and make sure the box was back in its original position.

"ANGUS!" Uncle Jeff hollered again from upstairs.

"COMING," I yelled as I began running out of my room toward the stairs.

As I approached the stairs, now in a full sprint, Uncle Jeff was coming down the stairs. We collided and the massive difference in weight caused me to go sailing backwards down the stairs. As I fell backwards, I hit my head against the hard concrete floor. I heard the loud thud as my skull bounced off the concrete. Blackness engulfed me.

Uncle Jeff woke me up by throwing a large glass of cold water on my face. I sat up too quickly and was extremely dizzy. The room was spinning. The back of my head burned.

"What the hell is your problem boy?" Uncle Jeff furiously stated.

I was just recently in a coma and had a brain injury from a severe car wreck that took my dad's life. I would have thought that my uncle would have called 9-1-1 when he seen me hit my head on the concrete and lose consciousness. At the very least, I would have thought that he would have been concerned that I may have reinjured my brain and would have shown me some compassion. If I had thought this, I would have been wrong! Uncle Jeff was furious with me because I didn't answer him the first time he called and because I ran into him as I was running in sheer trepidation up the stairs to answer his beckon.

"Are you deaf? Did you not hear me the first time I called your name?" Uncle Jeff screamed.

"I'm sorry, Uncle Jeff. I must have fell asleep when I got home from school. I came running as soon as I realized you were home and calling for me," I lied.

"Oh, while I'm still at work, Precious is home taking a nap!" Uncle Jeff said in a mocking baby-talk voice.

"I'm sorry. I'll make up for it," I pleaded.

Uncle Jeff came back, "You know what I think? I would appreciate some privacy tonight. My girlfriend Samantha is coming over for dinner. Since you didn't do your chores, you can skip dinner and stay in your room. That way, Sam and I can enjoy our dinner without your annoying presence!"

"Yes sir," I said and turned around and began walking back to my room.

"Stop right there, Princess!" Uncle Jeff stated after I got about three steps away.

"Yes sir?" I asked as I turned around and looked toward my uncle.

The sheer hatred in his eyes was terrifying.

"You said you came home from school and fell asleep?" Uncle Jeff asked.

I didn't realize where he was going with the question. "Yes, sir. I'm sorry. I haven't been feeling very well lately," I answered in a pitiful voice.

"Oh, you haven't been feeling very well?" Uncle Jeff answered mockingly.

"No sir," was all I could say.

"Well, I don't always feel well either. But, I go to work every single day! I'm guessing you didn't complete your chores when you came home."

I couldn't lie. I knew Uncle Jeff would find something. "No sir. I'll get started on them right now," I said hoping to appease my uncle.

"Oh, you'll do your chores. But not until after I whip your ass!" Uncle Jeff exclaimed as he began removing his belt.

I looked at my uncle in disbelief. My head was still throbbing from the fall. My heart was beating so fast that I thought it was going to beat right out of my chest.

"Walk your pitiful ass over to the couch, pull down your pants, and bend over!" Uncle Jeff ordered me.

I did as I was told.

Uncle Jeff hit me across my bare butt five times. The loud crack of the belt echoed throughout the house. I bit my lip and couldn't help but let out a slight whimper after every strike. Tears streamed down my face as I stared into the couch cushion. I'm not sure which was worse, the pain from the belt or the humiliation from bending over with my pants down.

After the fifth strike, Uncle Jeff said, "Now pull your pants up and do your chores like you should have done in the first place! Samantha will be here in an hour. You will be done with your chores before she gets here or you'll get your ass whipped again when she leaves!"

As I gingerly pulled my pants up, I felt blood trickling down the back of my legs. My jeans rubbing against my raw bottom made it very painful to walk. I did my best to ignore the excruciating pain and started on my chores.

I finished my chores before Samantha arrived. Uncle Jeff was in the kitchen preparing his and Samantha's dinner. I couldn't look at him. I was afraid to look at him.

As I was walking toward the stairs to go to the basement, Uncle Jeff said, "Hold on a minute!"

I froze. What had I done wrong now? "Yes sir?" I said looking down at Uncle Jeff's shoes rather than look him in the eyes.

"You can't go to bed without dinner. Can you?" Uncle Jeff replied.

"I am pretty hungry," I answered still without making eye contact.

"Of course you are. You haven't eaten since you came home from school. Here you are precious," Uncle Jeff responded as he handed me two slices of stale bread and a glass of water.

I probably should have been shocked. Perhaps my uncle was going for that effect. But, I was just happy to take the bread and water and get away from my uncle.

"Thank you, sir" I said as I took the items, turned around, and retreated to my dungeon.

I walked down the stairs. My bottom aching as my jeans rubbed up and down as I descended the steps. I walked over to my cot and laid down on my stomach. The image of me bending over with my pants down as my uncle viciously whipped me burned in my mind for about twenty minutes.

At first, I just laid there crying. I suppressed the sound of my crying in the pillow so my uncle wouldn't hear me. I just knew if he heard me crying he would get angry and come downstairs and beat me again.

I decided I wasn't helping myself by loathing in self-pity and dwelling on what I had just endured. I escaped and spent the night with Brian Robeson, the main character in my book *Hatchet*. I read for hours. While reading, I pretended that I was in the Canadian wilderness with Brian. Uncle Jeff could yell at me, demean me, intimidate me, and beat me. But, I always had my books to escape to! I fell asleep that night with one thing on my mind... ESCAPE!

Chapter 8

Saturday, October 26ᵗʰ, 2013 is a day that will be etched in my mind forever. It was unseasonably warm that day. The high was supposed to reach near eighty degrees.

Uncle Jeff awoke at 7:00 a.m. to get ready to go play in an all-day golf tournament. I asked him if I could stay the night with my friend Anthony. Surprisingly, he said I could, as long as I got all of the chores done that he had made me a list for. I couldn't believe what I had heard! I was actually going to be allowed to leave the house with Uncle Jeff's permission!

When I saw the list, I understood why he was so willing to let me go. I might have the chores done in ten hours if I was lucky. I was determined to follow through with my plan.

As soon as Uncle Jeff left, I sat down on one of the wingback chairs and called Anthony.

"Hello," Anthony's mother answered the phone.

"Hello Mrs. Simmons. This is Angus McGuire. May I speak to Anthony please?" I asked.

"Well hello Angus, honey I was so sorry to hear about your daddy. Are you doing ok sweetheart?" Anthony's mom asked.

"I'm getting by fine, Mrs. Simmons. Thank you very much for asking," I said trying to sound happy.

"You need to come see us, Angus! We miss having you around. Just a minute sweetie, I'll have to wake Anthony up. He's still sleeping," Mrs. Simmons replied.

"Thank you, ma'am," I said.

I waited for a few minutes before Anthony answered the phone.

"Hey buddy!" Anthony finally said in a sleepy voice.

"Hey pal! I got some good news!" I stated in a fake excited voice.

"What's up?" Anthony asked.

"My uncle says I can stay the night with you tonight as long as I get a massive list of chores done first!" I said with continued faked enthusiasm.

"Sweet! MOM, ANGUS IS STAYING THE NIGHT TONIGHT!" Anthony yelled to his mom.

I heard Anthony's mom ask in the background what time I would be coming over. Anthony told her I'd be there as soon as I was done with a massive amount of chores.

"Hey, I'll see you tonight buddy. I have to get started on this chore list!" I told Anthony.

"Do you need my mom to come pick you up?" Anthony asked.

"No, I would rather walk. I kind of enjoy walking since I got my cast off," I lied.

"Ok, my man. Just swing on by when you get done with your chores!" Anthony said excitedly.

I hung up and sat for a few minutes staring at the phone. Anthony was so excited. It had been months since I had been to his house. I could see Anthony sitting in his living room, with his Fedora on, watching out the front window for me to walk up to his house. How long would he sit there waiting for me to show up before he gave up and realized I wasn't coming? I knew my last conversation with my best friend was all one big lie. I knew the hurt he was going to feel. I also knew that I had just spoken to my best friend for the last time in my life. I was overwhelmed with sadness.

I looked at the clock. It was 7:59 a.m. I started on the chore list.

• • •

By noon, I had cleaned all of the windows inside and out, raked all of the leaves in the front and back yard, and swept the driveway, porch, and patio.

If anyone had seen the furious pace I was working at, they would have thought I was insane. I was working so fast that I was breathing heavy. At noon, I took five minutes to scarf down a ham and cheese sandwich and drink a glass of ice water and went back to work.

From 12:05 p.m. until 4 p.m. I cleaned out the gutters, trimmed the shrubs, swept the garage, and did all of the laundry. I worked like a maniac. I wanted to have all of the chores complete and be gone before Uncle Jeff came home.

I knew that if I didn't complete all of my chores perfectly, I stood the risk of raising suspicions with Uncle Jeff. From 4-4:30 I went back over the chore list and inspected my work. I walked all through the yard to make sure I didn't miss any leaves. I walked along the driveway, porch, and patio to make sure there was nothing on the pavement. I looked at the shrubs to make sure there was not a single twig out of proportion. I used a pair of scissors to correct a couple of blemishes. I inspected the garage floor to make sure it was immaculate. I made sure that every piece of clothing was folded neatly in the baskets. For good measure, I removed the lint trap from the dryer and washed it out with the sprayer on the kitchen sink. Of course, I wiped the sink dry when I was done so there were no water spots left behind. Everything looked perfect. Uncle Jeff (and the police) would be convinced that I had did my chores in fear of Uncle Jeff coming home and not approving. They would also be convinced that I had planned to come home.

I sat down at the kitchen table and wrote Uncle Jeff a note:

I'm walking to Anthony's house to spend the night.

I'll be home tomorrow to do my chores.

Angus

I quickly showered and wiped the shower dry when I was done. I put on a pair of blue jeans, my field boots, a solid black sweatshirt with a white t-shirt underneath, my woodland camo jacket, the "Tommy Lee wig", and a solid black baseball cap. I placed a thick black sock cap in the pocket of my jacket. It was very warm that day, but I figured I'd need that jacket and the sock cap when it did get cold and I needed somewhere to hide the petroleum jelly, coffee mug, and my notebook with all of my survival tips.

With the petroleum jelly, coffee mug, and notebook tucked under my coat, I started walking as if I was walking to Anthony's house. I kept my head down and stared at the pavement in front of me as I walked. The brim from the hat blocked my face from any possible onlookers.

A McDonald's restaurant sat about three blocks from Uncle Jeff's house. I casually walked through the McDonald's parking lot. I quickly looked around to make sure no one was paying any attention to me. I did not see anyone.

Behind every McDonald's restaurant is an enclosed dumpster where the employees take out the trash. My dad had worked for McDonald's when he was a teenager. He had told me a story about a time he had found some homeless people going through the dumpster getting the hamburgers out of the trash that McDonald's threw away. I went into the dumpster area and climbed into the dumpster. Luckily, the dumpster was about half-full of trash bags when I climbed in. I fell into the dumpster and landed softly on top of the trash bags. I stripped out of my clothes and smeared petroleum jelly over every inch of my body.

Next, I put my clothes back on over my now jelly covered body. It wasn't the most pleasant feeling, but it had to be done.

Finally, I laid down on top of some full trash bags and waited for darkness to fall.

While I was waiting, a teenage boy came out to the dumpster to deposit trash. The dumpster was about six feet tall and I was laying down in the bottom of it. There was no way the boy could see me. However, I didn't anticipate the large bags of trash being hurled into the dumpster. The first one caught me by surprise. I was laying on my back when all of a sudden I saw the big bag of trash come flying over the side of the dumpster. WHAM! The first bag of trash hit me right on top of my head. It didn't hurt much, but it did scare the crap out of me! I let out an "OOOMMMFFF" when the bag struck my head.

I heard the young boy say, "Hello? Is somebody there?"

I kept quiet. Three more trash bags came hurling into the dumpster. I rolled over on my stomach. One of the three remaining trash bags hit me in the back. The other two missed. I didn't make another sound.

After the boy left, I decided that it might be a good idea to take some food with me. I opened one of the trash bags and was shocked to find an overabundance of uneaten cooked food. There were cooked hamburger patties, chicken nuggets, fish fillets, French fries, and even some apple pies!

The hamburger patties were greasy, so I stuffed my coat full of chicken nuggets, fish fillets, and some of the apple pies. I had enough food to survive for several days now!

Darkness fell around 6:30. I peeked over the dumpster to make sure there was no one around. I saw several cars lined up around the drive thru. I knew there was a good chance that someone would see me climb out of the dumpster. But, they would assume that I was a homeless vagrant that had simply climbed in the dumpster for a free meal! I had to get out from under the parking lot lights as quickly as possible. I immediately went behind the dumpster to the open field, away from the bright lights and began my long walk.

I had to stay close to the main roads. I could have made much better time if I traveled "as the crow flies". But, I didn't know my way except by the roads. So, I simply walked through the weeds alongside the road.

It had cooled off quite a bit since the sun went down, but I began to get hot and sweat. I suppose the jelly that was covering my entire body didn't allow my pores to release my perspiration adequately or perhaps it impeded the evaporation process that allowed my body to efficiently cool itself and regulate my body temperature. I took off my coat and carried it.

My skin was slimy from the combination of petroleum jelly and sweat. The wig was making my head itch terribly. But, I didn't dare take it off. If anyone saw me, they would see a strange looking man with long hair. They would not see a young 13-year-old kid! I tried taking off my sweatshirt also, but I quickly became cold and had to put it back on. To say the walk was unpleasant would be an understatement. I was miserable.

After walking for approximately two hours, I came to the old country road that my dad had turned on. I was glad to reach this road. I knew this road was scarcely traveled, and since it was now close to nine o'clock at night, I might not see another person during my travels!

I walked along the old country road for what seemed like forever. I'm guessing I actually walked for about three hours. While I was walking, I was wondering if Anthony had tried calling Uncle Jeff's house to see why I hadn't shown up at his house yet. If he had, Uncle Jeff was probably looking for me right then!

If Anthony had not called, then I had several more hours before Uncle Jeff would realize that I was missing. I really hoped that Anthony had not called. I don't think Uncle Jeff or the police would be looking for me in this direction. They would most likely center their search on the route from

Uncle Jeff's house to Anthony's house. If dogs were able to track my scent, they would track me to the McDonalds and assume that I had simply stopped there for a burger or something. Hopefully, the petroleum jelly worked and the dogs would lose my scent around the dumpster and the police would assume that I had been abducted on the McDonald's parking lot.

After much walking and a lot of nervous worrying, I reached the gravel road. Luckily, for me, there was a full moon that night. If there had not been, I probably would not have been able to see to walk.

When you get away from all of the lights in town, it's amazing how much different the sky looks at night. I looked up as I walked. I could see thousands of stars in the sky. The rocks crackled under my feet as I walked. Each side of the road was lined with trees. I stopped momentarily and just stared at the stars. I looked up to the brightest star in the sky and said aloud, "I'm going to our cave, Dad. I know you'll be with me in spirit." I wasn't sad when I said this. I actually felt very peaceful.

I finally came to the field that Dad had drove across. I figured I was safe from being seen, so, I removed my wig, scratched my head for several seconds, and shoved the wig in my coat pocket. I planned to burn the wig later.

I abandoned the gravel road and began walking across the field. The grass in the field was about waist high. I didn't walk for very long before I came to the forest that Dad and I had entered.

Upon arriving at the forest, I decided that I had better wait until daybreak before trying to navigate the forest. I have an excellent sense of direction, but I knew that there was a better than good chance that I would get lost if I tried to walk the woods at night.

I sat down beside a large white oak tree and ate a few of the chicken nuggets from my coat pocket. I was extremely thirsty and immediately regretted eating the nuggets. Why hadn't I brought a bottle of water in my coat? I knew there were numerous creeks on the way to the cave in the woods. I would be able to get water soon! I sat, waited, and wondered if anybody knew I was gone yet.

Chapter 9

I'm not sure what time I fell asleep. When I woke up, the Sun was halfway up in the eastern sky. I guessed it was around 9 a.m. The events of the previous day had obviously worn me out.

As I stood up, I realized that sleeping in the wilderness was going to take some getting used to. My whole body ached. My legs were sore from all of the walking. My shoulders and back ached from all of the chores I had done at Uncle Jeff's house. My neck hurt so bad that I couldn't turn my head to the right. This must have been due to my awkward sleeping position against the giant white oak tree. I began my walk.

As I walked, the soreness and stiffness in my body gradually went away, except for my neck! I had to turn my whole body to look to my right.

I came to a creek. By this time, I was beyond thirsty. But, during my research, I had read about the importance of purifying water before drinking it. I filled my coffee mug up with water from the creek, but I didn't drink it. I kept trekking.

I came to my dad's clubhouse. I now looked at the clubhouse with different eyes. After getting to know my uncle, I tried to envision my dad and him working together to build the clubhouse. What had caused my uncle to become the man that he was now? He was the exact opposite of my dad! My dad was kind, generous, and never had a cross word to say to anyone. My uncle was cold-hearted and just plain mean! I had to stop thinking about my uncle! Every time I thought about him, my stomach would churn and my heart would beat a little faster. I moved on.

I hiked up several embankments and crossed the creek that meandered through the woods several more times. After about thirty minutes, I saw the boulder. I smiled as soon as I saw it.

I envisioned my dad and MacGyver walking with me as I approached it.

"Glad you finally made it!" My imaginary dad said to me with a wink and a grin.

"Me too!" I said aloud.

Imaginary MacGyver wagged his tail and let out a "woof" of enthusiasm.

I went behind the boulder and crawled into the cave. The backpack was still where dad had left it. I took off my clothes and used the t-shirt to wipe the petroleum jelly off my body. I turned my clothes inside out so the petroleum jelly wouldn't be touching my body, and put them back on. I opened the backpack and retrieved the magnesium fire starter. I had to boil the water to drink!

I wish I could say that I had a roaring fire going in no time. However, that was not the case. I didn't have any problem finding plenty of firewood. There was an abundance of sticks for kindling. I found several fallen trees that were rotted enough that I was able to break large limbs off for my fire. I also gathered some dry leaves and dry grass.

Behind the bolder, in front of my cave entrance, I dug a small hole about four feet in diameter and about three inches deep. Next, I placed three small flat rocks in the center of the hole in a triangular fashion. I would use these rocks to set my coffee mug with water. I crumbled up some leaves and placed them loosely in the bottom of the hole in between and around the rocks. I added some dry grass on top of the leaves. I took my magnesium fire starter and shaved off some of the magnesium on top of the dry grass. Finally, I began scraping the fire rod on the flint to cause sparks to fly down and hit the magnesium shavings on top of the dry grass.

I saw the embers ignite several times but I was unable to produce a flame. I began to get frustrated. *Why wasn't the dry grass catching fire?*

I stopped for a few minutes and thought about what I was doing. I had dry leaves and dry grass. Both were so dry that they would easily crumble when I squeezed them in my hand. I didn't have them packed too tight, so there was plenty of room for oxygen to circulate throughout.

That's it! I wasn't blowing on the embers. I felt dumb when I realized I had forgot this simple step in starting the fire.

I struck the fire rod to the flint two more times and I had an ember glowing on the dry grass. I put my face close to the ember and gently blew. The grass burst into a flame almost immediately. I carefully added more dry grass on top of the flame. I gently blew some more until this grass was burning. Next, I began adding small twigs gradually. Finally, I added the larger pieces of wood that I had gathered. I used a long stick to place my coffee mug in the center of the fire on top of the rocks.

Within about fifteen minutes, my water was boiling. I allowed the water to boil for about two minutes to ensure it was purified. Finally, I used the stick to carefully remove the coffee mug from the fire without spilling my water. I let the water set for about five minutes to let it cool enough to drink. Then, I drank my water. This water was quite possibly the best water I had ever drunk in my life! After drinking the water, I immediately felt much better. I had obviously been dehydrated and not really realized it!

I spent a couple of hours bringing firewood into my cave. I figured it was a good idea to store firewood inside my cave just in case it rained so I would always have dry wood for a fire. This would have been much easier if the entrance to my cave was bigger. I would throw the pieces of wood into the entrance until they piled up so much that I couldn't throw any more in. Then, I would have to crawl in and move them. I chose the right side of my cave for my wood supply. I knew that winter was very close and I would need a lot of wood for the winter. I also knew that when the weather got cold I wouldn't want to get out much to get more firewood. Therefore, I decided I would work every day stocking up on wood. My goal was to stack the entire length of the wall with firewood until it was as tall as I was. I munched on my McDonald's food supply throughout the day.

It was getting close to dawn when I realized I hadn't made me a bed inside my cave yet. This was a mistake on my part. After all of my research, I had failed to consider this. I was exhausted and ready to lay down. But, I needed a bed to sleep on.

I began looking around for bedding material. I used my sweatshirt to carry as many dry leaves into my cave as I could. I would build a platform for my bed later! I worked until my pile of leaves was around six feet long by three feet wide and about two feet deep.

I built up the fire in my fire pit outside of my cave. The boulder acted as a natural heat shield that directed the heat from the fire back into my cave. I was also hoping the fire would ward off any mountain lions, bears, or any other predatory animal that might wander by my cave, get a whiff of me, and decide that I would make a good meal.

I sat outside my new home next to the fire looking at the stars for a while. The flames from my fire flickered and danced. The wood popped as it burned. My mind drifted back to all of the events that had happened over the past several weeks. As I sat watching the flames from my fire underneath the clear starlit night, I realized that I had absolutely no regrets about my decision. I thought about my dad. I knew my dad would have been proud of me. I missed my dad immensely, but this felt right. I returned to my new home and slept better that first night than I had since the accident.

Chapter 10

*J*eff McGuire played golf all day on Saturday, October 26 2013. Anthony Simmons did not call him to ask where Angus was. Anthony knew how Angus's uncle was and assumed that he had found an excuse to keep Angus trapped at his house to do more chores.

Jeff McGuire pulled into his driveway at precisely 6 p.m. He had no idea that at this very time his nephew was lying in a dumpster being pelted with flying trash bags.

As Jeff got out of his truck, he looked around the yard scanning for leaves. He didn't see a single leaf in his yard. He made a circle around his house looking for any type of smudge or streak on any of his windows. The windows were spotless. He walked the entire length of his driveway and carefully examined the porch and patio. They were all immaculate. He looked at his shrubs. The shrubs were all neatly trimmed. He looked underneath his shrubs. There, underneath the shrubs, he found what he was looking for. Angus had neatly raked all of the clippings away from the shrubs, but he had failed to get the clippings from underneath the shrubs.

Jeff smiled and thought, *"I got you now you little bastard!"*

Jeff went into his garage and inspected the floor. It was perfect! Jeff walked into the house hoping to find Angus so he could scold him. He did not. Instead, he saw the note on the kitchen table.

I'm walking to Anthony's house to spend the night.

I'll be home tomorrow to do my chores.

Angus

"Oh you will definitely do your chores tomorrow!" Jeff thought to himself with an evil smile across his face.

Jeff went into the laundry room and saw that all of his laundry was done, and his clothes were folded neatly inside a laundry basket. Jeff went to the fridge, drank his 18th beer for the day, and went to bed.

Jeff slept until 10 o'clock the next morning. He was hungover and had a severe headache. He walked through the house to see if Angus had come home yet. Angus was nowhere to be found.

"What was that princess's friend's name?" Jeff thought to himself. He couldn't remember so he went to his phone and simply hit "redial".

"Hello?" a woman's voice answered on the other end.

"Yes ma'am, this is Jeff McGuire. I'm looking for my nephew, Anthony. Do I have the right number?" Jeff asked in a fake polite voice.

"Um, yes, Mr. McGuire. I think you have the correct number. This is Ann Simmons. I'm Anthony's mom. Angus was supposed to come over last night, but he never showed up. Is he not at home with you?" the lady replied.

For once in his life, Jeff McGuire became worried.

"No ma'am. Angus is not home. He left me a note saying he was going to your house last night," Uncle Jeff responded with a hint of worry escaping from his voice.

"Oh, no. I sure hope Angus is alright!" Mrs. Simmons said.

"This is not like Angus. I better call the police!" Jeff McGuire stated trying to sound genuinely concerned. If something had happened to Angus, Jeff knew that his plan could be ruined. He could not let that happen!

The police were dispatched to Jeff McGuire's house. Officer James Mullins arrived at 10:25 a.m. Jeff told Officer Mullins how he had been gone all day the previous day playing in a charity golf tournament. He left out the part about drinking all day and stumbling home and sleeping off a hangover. Officer Mullins asked if Jeff had noticed anything unusual in Angus's behavior or if any of his belongings were missing. Jeff said that he had not noticed anything unusual. He said that Angus had spent the previous day doing a few chores around the house. He showed Officer Mullins the note that Angus had left. He took Officer Mullins to Angus's room and verified that nothing was missing. He added that Angus had only been staying with him for a short time and that he was working on getting Angus a nice bedroom suite and a proper bed. Of course, that was a lie. Jeff did not intend to get anything for Angus. In fact, Jeff had planned to execute his plan tonight to get rid of Angus for good. Officer Mullins asked if Angus had any other relatives that would want to take Angus. Jeff told the officer that he was Angus's only surviving relative.

"I don't think your nephew is a runaway. If he was going to run away, he wouldn't have done his chores and he would have taken some of his belongings," Officer Mullins informed Jeff.

"Ok, so what do we do now?" Jeff asked doing his best to sound like a caring uncle.

"We know where Angus was heading. I will make a call and get a K-9 unit over here to see if they can pick up his trail. I will also be questioning your neighbors to see if they can provide us with any insight. I'll be issuing an Amber Alert. This will get the word out to everyone with an enabled cellphone, news media, and all law enforcement nationwide. I know this is a stressful time, Mr. McGuire, but, try to remain calm," Officer Mullins stated and he quickly returned to his patrol car.

None of the neighbors was much help to the police. One neighbor, Ms. Turner, informed the police that she had seen a strange looking man with long black hair walking down the street around 5 p.m.

The K-9 unit from a nearby correctional facility was dispatched to Jeff's house to attempt to pick up Angus's scent. The dogs were able to track the scent to a nearby McDonald's, but lost the scent on the parking lot. The K-9 officer informed Officer Mullins that he believed Angus must have gotten into a vehicle with someone on the parking lot. He said that the dogs had a strong scent until they reached the parking lot.

Officer Mullins interviewed the manager at McDonalds, Paul Sisk, to see if the parking lot had been sprayed or cleaned recently. Sisk said that the parking lots were cleaned Friday morning and had not been cleaned again since. Officer Mullins asked Sisk if they had any security cameras. Sisk said that they did, but unfortunately, the camera's recorders were not working.

All employees from the previous night were interviewed. A Friday night at McDonald's is a very busy night. None of the employees stated that they had noticed anything out of the ordinary. The only lead that Officer Mullins had was the neighbor's statement about a strange looking man with long hair walking down the street. It did not look good!

• • •

Amber Dunn was driving to work at when the Amber Alert went off on her phone. She looked at the alert and read in disbelief as she read:

ACTIVE AMBER ALERT

Missing Child in Park Hills, MO.

Angus McGuire was last seen on Friday. Please call (573) 555-1989 if you see this child.

A picture of Angus was in the corner of the screen next to the text. Amber pulled over to the side of the road, reread the text, and stared at the picture in disbelief.

Amber punched the quick dial key to her work on her cellphone and informed her supervisor that she had a family emergency and that she was not going to be able to come in today.

Amber was glad she had taken the time to write down Jeff McGuire's address when he had signed Angus out of the hospital against the doctor's strong recommendation that Angus stay several days longer. Amber entered the address in her phone's GPS and headed to Park Hills.

Amber had a bad feeling about Jeff McGuire the moment she met him. There was something not right about him. She accelerated to 80 miles per hour as her mind continued to worry and wonder where Angus was at this very minute!

• • •

Amber pulled in front of Jeff McGuire's house at 11:45 a.m. There was a police cruiser setting in the driveway. What was Amber going to say? Should she simply walk up to a police officer and say, *"Hello officer, I'm Amber Dunn. I took care of Angus while he was in the hospital. I met his uncle and got a bad vibe from him. I think he is a psychopath. Can you please tell me what you know about where Angus might be?"*

Amber also thought it was a bad idea to confront Jeff McGuire. That guy gave her the creeps! She decided it would be best for her to go to the police station and talk to the police, but leave out her psychopath theory.

Amber was able to find the police station by using Google on her phone. She pulled into the police station and saw an officer getting out of his cruiser. Amber quickly approached the officer.

"Excuse me sir...," Amber said as she walked quickly toward the officer.

"Yes, ma'am. Can I help you?" answered the officer.

"I'm a friend of Angus McGuire's. I was wondering if I could get some information about his disappearance," replied Amber.

"I'm not allowed to disclose much information ma'am. All I can tell you is that right now we are treating the case as a possible kidnapping," the officer replied and walked hurriedly into the police station.

Amber noticed the officer's nametag was "Mullins". Amber didn't know what to think. A possible kidnapping? All kinds of things ran through Amber's mind. Amber remembered reading about the case of Shawn Hornbeck. Shawn Hornbeck was kidnapped when he was eleven. Four years later, Shawn was found alive. He had been kidnapped and held captive by Michael Devlin. Could something like this have happened to Angus? Amber couldn't bear the thought of it!

Amber walked back to her car and cried. She thought about those three weeks that she had spent taking care of Angus while he was in his coma. She remembered watching through the door as the doctor told Angus's uncle that there was a good chance Angus would never wake up from his coma. She had seen Jeff turn away from the doctor, smile when the doctor told him this, and then feign to start crying. Amber decided that she didn't believe Angus had been kidnapped. Jeff McGuire had something to do with Angus's disappearance! She was determined to find out what!

Amber thought about telling her suspicions to the police right then. But, then a cold fear came upon her. She was afraid if Jeff had done something to Angus, he might do something to her to keep her quiet.

Amber sat in her car to gather her thoughts. She thought back to her last phone conversation with Angus. It was obvious that Angus was not happy. Amber could sense the fear in Angus's voice. He seemed rushed to hang up the phone. Perhaps he was afraid his uncle would catch him talking on the phone. Maybe he was forbidden from using the phone. Angus hadn't said much. *But, he did mention taking me to see his cave!* Amber thought.

Why were the police treating this like a kidnapping? Could Angus have run away to his cave? The last thing that Angus and his dad had talked about was spending a week in the woods in a cave. It made perfect sense that Angus had run away to his dad's cave! The police didn't know about the cave. As far as Amber knew, nobody besides her and Angus knew about the cave. Maybe the police were right and Angus had been kidnapped. Amber didn't think so. Amber had a feeling she knew exactly where Angus could be found. But, should she tell anyone about her suspicions? This was something she was going to have to take time and think about.

Chapter 11

*A*fter sleeping on my hastily made bed of leaves, I realized the importance of making a bed up off the ground. My fire beside the large boulder did an amazing job of radiating the heat back into my cave. The side of my body facing toward the fire was very warm. However, the cold from the ground underneath the leaves kept one side of my body chilled all night.

My Swiss Army knife, that dad had left, had a small saw blade on it. I used this to cut down six small cedar trees. The small saw blade on the knife worked superbly. I had the trees cut down in little over an hour.

Next, I cut all of the limbs off the trees. This took about another hour to accomplish. I cut two of the trees down to be six feet long and laid them parallel to each other inside my cave close to the entrance. I spread them about three feet apart. I placed all of the leaves I had used for my bed in between these two "logs".

Next, I cut the remaining four trees into four feet "logs". I cut notches into the parallel logs and placed the four logs across the parallel logs and on top of the leaves. Now I had a natural airflow between the ground and my bed. My body would not be losing heat to the cold ground. I gathered more leaves and stuffed them in between the log slats to provide some cushioning. My bed was now complete.

I laid down and I was impressed at how comfortable my bed was. The small entrance to my cave kept the inside of my cave warm. The heat that I was able to radiate from my fire should keep my cave warm, even when winter came. However, I may still want a blanket of some kind when it got really cold, or when the rain didn't allow me to build a fire outside. I would tackle this problem soon. Right now, I decided to go find the river that Dad had mentioned.

I gathered the fishing line, the sinkers, and the hooks and started walking north. Dad was right. I walked for approximately ten minutes and came to a river. I heard the river before I saw it. I was amazed at how quickly I had become in tune with nature.

When you are in the woods, you quickly start noticing sounds that you did not pay attention to before. I noticed the squirrels barking in the trees, the birds singing, the leaves crunching underneath my feet, and I noticed the sound of running water when I approached the river.

The forest opened up into a clearing and I saw the river. The river wasn't real big. It was only about thirty yards wide. There were trees along each side of it with branches that hung out over the river. I immediately thought about the fishing method I had read about. I would definitely be trying the fishing line on the tree limb method here! However, today I simply wanted to catch my first fish and eat something besides stale McDonald's food!

I found a small branch about six feet long and used my Swiss Army knife to cut it off a Maple tree. I cut a small notch in the end of the branch and tied a strand of fishing line about twelve feet long to it. I attached a spit sinker about four feet from the end of the line and used my teeth to squeeze it together. Finally, I tied a hook to the end of the line. Now, I simply had to find some bait. I laid my homemade fishing pole down beside the river and began my quest for bait.

My research had provided me with numerous tips of where to find bait. Right now, I wanted the easiest and simplest way. I began looking for a rotting stump. A rotting stump often contained grub worms. If I was desperate, I could also eat the grub worms as a good source of protein. I wasn't desperate!

I walked along the riverbank and came to a dead tree. The tree had been dead for some time and was beginning to rot. I found a large rock and used the rock to chip away at the base of the tree. I had only struck the tree with the rock four or five times when I found my first grub. *Wow! That was easy!* I thought. I grabbed the grub and ran back to where I had left my fishing pole. I placed the grub on the hook and threw it out into the river.

The current caused the grub to drift downriver. I was surprised at how quickly I got a bite. About the time all of the slack from my line was out, I felt a strong pull on my pole. I quickly yanked, and began pulling in my first fish. I didn't have an actual fishing reel to reel in the fish. I didn't want to grab the fishing line. I had made that mistake once when I went fishing with my dad when I was about nine years old. The fishing line had sliced through my hand and cut me. It was very painful, almost like a paper cut. Instead of grabbing the line with my hand, I simply walked backwards.

When I had the fish on the bank, I placed my foot on top of it. The fish wasn't huge. But, it wasn't small either. It was a smallmouth bass. It was about twelve inches long. I used my rock to hit the fish in the head to kill it so it wouldn't continue flopping around.

I knew from my survival research that at this point, I could have gutted the fish and continued fishing with the fish's entrails. However, I was excited to cook my first fish. So, I gutted the fish in the river and simply threw the entrails into the water. My Swiss Army knife also had a fish-scaling tool on it. I removed all of the scales from the fish and cut off its head. I did all of this in the shallow water of the river. I ran excitedly back to my cave.

Upon returning to the entrance to my cave, I sat my soon to be meal down on a rock. I decided

I wanted to jazz up my meal with some wild onions.

As I walked away from my cave to search for some wild onions to add to my fish, I saw a large hawk swoop down toward my cave. I watch helplessly as the large bird snatched up my fish and flew away. I stood watching in disbelief. My excitement about my first real survival meal quickly turned to anger.

"NOOOOOOOOOO!" I yelled, as the bird continued to fly away. *That didn't really just happen!* I thought.

I returned to the rotting tree again in search for grubs. This time it wasn't so easy. I chipped away at the rotting tree for fifteen to twenty minutes before I was able to find a grub. I again put the grub on my hook and threw it to the center of the river.

I'm not sure if it was the blood from the previous fish that had scared the fish away or if perhaps, the fish had simply moved elsewhere in the river. Whatever it was, I was unable to catch another fish that day. It had been so easy the first time.

After about an hour, I gave up on my quest to catch another fish. I returned home and ate the rest of my stale McDonald's and boiled some water to drink. I learned quickly that a positive state of mind is crucial in wilderness survival. I was really down after I lost my first fish to the hawk. However, I realized that the hawk was simply surviving just like me. I decided that the next day I would try my luck with the slingshot.

Chapter 12

I awoke the next morning famished. Something else that I learned quickly was that when you are surviving in the wilderness you constantly have to work for everything. This burns many calories and you are always hungry.

I had planned to spend some time practicing with the slingshot, but I was so hungry that I decided to forego the practice and try to quickly kill something to eat. I gathered several marble-sized rocks and began walking through the forest in search of game.

I tried repeatedly to hit a squirrel. Squirrels don't provide a very big target and you can't get very close to them. I could not hit a squirrel with my slingshot. I foolishly shot at several birds, also. I didn't come close to hitting any of them. I probably spent two hours trying to hit something with my slingshot to no avail. I should have taken the time to practice.

By the time I realized that my slingshot hunting was completely futile, I was weak from hunger. My McDonald's food supply was gone. I didn't want to risk going fishing again and not catching any. Therefore, I decided I would eat the food that was the easiest to find. I could choose from edible plants, berries, or insects. I decided I would search for edible plants or berries and if I happened to come across any insects during my search then I would eat them.

I had only been searching for about three minutes when I noticed a large grasshopper sitting on a tall blade of grass. I remembered reading that the best time to catch grasshoppers was during the early morning because they moved much slower during the cool mornings. It wasn't early morning, but I had to try. I slowly crept up toward the grasshopper. I would slowly take a step and then stop and freeze for several seconds. I did this several times. It took me ten minutes to get within a few feet of the grasshopper. My patience paid off. I got about two feet away from the grasshopper and just when I was slowly bending over, the grasshopper took flight. I reflexively swatted at the grasshopper and luckily knocked it to the ground. The grasshopper was momentarily dazed and I bent over and picked it up. This was no small grasshopper! I never thought about how big grasshoppers are, but this one was about as long and big around as my index finger.

I held the grasshopper right behind its head and looked at it. I knew the grasshopper was going to be crunchy when I ate it. I decided it was best not to dwell on how it was going to taste and instead quickly shoved it into my mouth and began chewing. I was right. The grasshopper was crunchy. I tried to trick my mind by trying to visualize that I was eating crunchy fried chicken. This helped a little. As soon as I bit down onto the grasshopper, a warm liquid released from inside the grasshopper into my mouth. The grasshopper tasted a little bit like peanut chicken. The taste actually wasn't bad. However, the juice from the grasshopper's guts shooting into my mouth when

I chewed was disgusting. I had anticipated this, but I still almost vomited. I figured that I'd get used to it.

I didn't see any more grasshoppers, but I did notice an old tree stump that I hadn't noticed before. I wondered if it was left over from one of the trees that my dad had cut down for his clubhouse.

I found a large rock and began chipping away at the stump. This stump must have been delicious for grubs because it was full of them. I found six large grubs in this one stump! I grabbed the first one, plopped it into my mouth, and quickly began chewing. The squishing and release of liquids gave me the same gagging reaction as before; however, I discovered that I actually enjoyed the taste of the grub. They almost tasted like almonds.

I quickly scarfed down three more and put the other two in my pocket. I decided I had enough bugs in my belly to hold me over and figured I would give fishing another try.

As I approached the river, I noticed something floating down the river toward me. At first, I thought it was a boat. As it came closer, I saw that it was a large black inner tube. I guessed that someone had been floating on it at some point in the river and had lost control of it. It was hard telling how far the inner tube had come. I immediately realized that the inner tube might come in handy.

I took my boots off and prepared for the cold water. I had myself all pumped up to dive into the cold water and retrieve the inner tube, when I noticed the current bringing the inner tube toward the bank. I only had to wade out from the bank about six feet and the inner tube floated straight to me. I snatched the inner tube from the water and took it over to the bank.

What kind of uses would I get from this inner tube? Would I use it to fish from like a boat? Perhaps I could use it to improve my bed. I could use it to cover the entrance to my cave to block out the cold air if it would fit. The possible uses of this inner tube were endless!

I pulled the inner tube far away from the bank so there was no chance the water would rise up and take it away.

I had to quit thinking about the luck of finding the inner tube and start fishing! I took one of the grubs from my pocket and put it on my fishing pole. I threw the line into the water.

Just like my first cast the previous day, right when the slack got out of my line, a fish took my bait. I jerked the pole. My pole bent a lot more than it did the previous day, and I had to struggle to hold on! I was afraid my line might break, so I didn't immediately start walking backwards to bring the fish in. Instead, I actually slowly walked forward into the water. My homemade pole was now almost completely bent in half. I really thought the pole or my line was going to break. Neither one did.

After what seemed like an eternity, I felt the pulling on the line decrease. I started walking backward. After I took three steps, the fish seemed to have gotten its second wind and began fighting again. Again, I moved forward. I repeated this process an additional five times before I finally landed the fish. I was ecstatic when I got the fish on the bank and saw it. The fish was a blue catfish. It was around thirty inches long. Again, I put my foot on top of it, hit it with a rock, and picked it up.

I had planned to attempt to catch two or three fish, but after seeing the size of this one, I decided this would be plenty.

In case you don't know, you don't clean catfish the same way that you do most fish. Most fish have scales that you simply scrape off (unless you are fileting them). Catfish on the other hand, have skin. You can't scrape it off. You have to pull it off.

My dad had taught me how to skin a catfish when I was nine years old. He had used a special set of pliers designed specifically for skinning catfish. I didn't have any pliers. I laid the fish down on a flat rock and cut off its tail to let it bleed out. My dad had taught me to do this just in case the fish wasn't dead. If you started cutting on a fish that you thought was dead, and it flopped while you were cutting, you could cut yourself!

I began gutting the catfish and thinking about how I was going to skin it. I could only think of one way. I was going to have to use my teeth. The first step in skinning a catfish is to remove its fins. If I had pliers, I would have used them to hold the fins while I cut them off. I didn't have any pliers. I couldn't use my teeth because I wouldn't have been able to see to cut. Therefore, I used a couple of flat rocks, held the fins between them with one hand, and cut the fins off with the other hand.

Next, I cut through the skin behind the head all the way around the fish. Then, I found a tree branch with a point sticking up from it and hung the fish up by its gills. I cut a slit all the way down the fishes back. Finally, I bit down on the skin at the top of the fish behind its head and peeled the skin off the fish with my teeth. It actually wasn't as hard as it may sound. The skin came off rather easily. The hardest part was getting it started. Once the skin started peeling away from the fish, it was a piece of cake. I had to skin each side of the fish separately. The whole process of skinning the catfish probably took less than ten minutes. I left the head on the fish when I was done to make it easier to carry.

When I got back to my cave, I decided the wild garlic was still a good idea. I just had to be smart and not leave my fish out in the open. I carried the fish inside my cave and placed it inside my backpack. I then went back out to find some wild onions. Wild onions are extremely easy to find. I found and harvested ten wild onions in a matter of minutes. I didn't even bother washing off the dirt. I wiped off what I could with my hands and figured that was good enough. I had actually read that a little dirt in your diet was good for you. Think about it. Do animals wash off their food in the wild? NO! The main reason we are taught to wash our food is because of all the chemicals that are put on them either to grow them or to preserve them. You don't have to worry about harsh fertilizers or chemicals in the wild.

I found several sticks and fashioned a crude spit to cook my fish. I knew that due to the thickness of this fish, it would be better cooked in a rotisserie fashion.

I cut up the fish into two large slabs of meat and put the wild onions in between. Next, I stuck small sticks through the sides of the two pieces of meat to hold it together. Finally, I stuck a long stick long ways through the two pieces of fish and sat the stick on top of my homemade spit over my fire.

When cooking with a spit, you have to have your meat several inches from the fire; otherwise, your spit itself will catch fire. My fish was approximately sixteen inches from the flames of the fire. The smell of the wild onions seeping into the fish meat as it cooked caused my mouth to continuously water while I waited for my meal to cook.

I would turn the spit about every five minutes. It took about forty-five minutes to cook my fish. I finally removed the fish from the fire and sat the sticks on top of the boulder.

I looked to the sky to ensure there were no hawks nearby waiting on a home-cooked meal. I let the fish cool for a couple of minutes and then held the stick up and bit directly into the fish off the stick. Perhaps it was because I was starving and had been eating grasshoppers and grubs. Perhaps cooking in the wild really is the best way to enjoy food. Whatever the reason, this fish was the most delicious fish I had ever eaten in my life. The juices of the meat exploded with flavor as I chewed. The wild onions added just the right amount of flavor to the tender fish meat. I savored every bite of the fish.

By the time I was done eating, I felt so full that I thought my stomach was going to pop. I placed my homemade spit beside my fire to use again later, added some more large pieces of wood to my fire so it would burn for several hours, and crawled inside my cave and fell asleep full, content, and happy.

Chapter 13

*J*eff McGuire woke up on Monday, October 28th, 2013 legitimately worried about his nephew, Angus. Jeff called his lead supervisor and reported that he had a family matter to attend to and that he would not be in his office today. He told him to call his cellphone only if the matter was urgent.

Jeff, with the help of his girlfriend Samantha, had been planning for weeks to kill Angus. Jeff's parents had left his brother close to four million dollars in their will. They had not left him a single dime. Jeff knew that they definitely had a good reason to not leave him as much as they had left his brother. But, to not leave him anything? This infuriated Jeff. The thought of Angus getting the money when he turned eighteen was too much for Jeff to bare. The only way he was going to see a dime of that inheritance was if Mike and Angus were both deceased.

The plan had been a simple one. After Angus had awoken from his coma and was still in the hospital, Jeff had taken his girlfriend, Samantha Tillman, to Elephant Rocks State Park in Belleview, Missouri, where he formulated his master plan.

Jeff and Samantha hiked the trail and came to a large rock ledge that overlooked the forest below. The rock ledge was about four hundred square feet in area. It was about a hundred feet above the forest floor. The leaves on the trees below were starting to change colors. The view from the ledge was breathtaking!   Samantha was exhilarated by the height of the rock ledge.

As Samantha stood at the edge, her heart began pounding rapidly as she stared at the tops of the trees far below. Samantha felt the surge of adrenaline course through her body as she stood staring at God's awesome creation. She stood there, unable to look away, as she relished the rush from the view.

Jeff McGuire stood about ten feet behind Samantha. As he stood watching Samantha in her hypnotic trance, he thought about how easy it would be to shove her off the ledge of the cliff. There were absolutely no witnesses around. All he had to do was give her a little shove and she would plummet to a certain death. It would be the perfect murder.

A smile spread across Jeff's face when he realized that he had the perfect plan. He had been trying to think of a way to kill Angus for days so he could get the inheritance that he felt was rightfully his. Now, the perfect plan had presented itself to him. Jeff could almost see Angus standing at the ledge looking on instead of Samantha. He envisioned shoving Angus. He could hear Angus scream in terror as he fell. He imagined Angus bouncing off the trees as he continued to fall and hit the ground with a loud thud. These thoughts gave Jeff great pleasure. Jeff's heart also began pounding rapidly and he too felt an adrenaline rush.

Jeff hadn't told Samantha about his evil thoughts while she was on the ledge with him. However, he had told her on the drive home about his plan. Samantha hadn't liked the idea of murder, but, she did like the idea of sharing four million dollars with Jeff. She had immediately started planning their wedding and honeymoon to the Bahamas. She had agreed to accompany Jeff and Angus on their hiking adventure so she could provide a witness's account to Angus's premature death.

Samantha agreed that she would state that she saw Angus get too close to the edge, slip on some loose gravel, and fall off. However, she stated that she couldn't watch it. She said she did not want the image of Jeff shoving Angus over the edge in her memory. Samantha was a smart girl. She realized that Jeff had formulated his plan while they were on the ledge together. This realization frightened Samantha.

Jeff had decided that he and Samantha would take Angus to Elephant Rocks on Sunday, October 27th. He hated to miss watching football, but he figured he could sacrifice one Sunday for four million dollars! Now his plan was possibly ruined- one day late! If Angus had been kidnapped, he wasn't sure if he'd ever see any of the money. Without a body, the money could be held in probate for a long time...possibly longer than Jeff was alive! The more Jeff thought about his current situation, the more furious he became.

Jeff was getting ready to head to the police station to see if the police had any new leads, when a thought came to his mind. What if Samantha thought that he had something to do with Angus's disappearance? Would she tell the police about their plan? Could he trust her? Why had he been foolish enough to tell her about his plan? Because he needed a witness to corroborate his statement after he shoved Angus over the ledge. That is why! He needed to get a feel on where Samantha's head was.

Jeff picked up his cellphone and called Samantha.

"Hello, Lover," Samantha answered her phone like she always did when Jeff called.

"Hey, Wildcat. With all this stuff going on with Angus, I took today off. You mind if I come over and talk for a bit?" Jeff asked.

He didn't sense anything out of the ordinary in Samantha's voice. In fact, she almost seemed too calm and normal considering the circumstances.

"I don't go into work until three today. I'm yours to do with as you please until then," Samantha flirtatiously replied.

Jeff didn't notice the two undercover police officers parked outside his house in the unmarked Dodge Charger. As Jeff climbed into his truck, Officer Mullins noted the time in his notebook of Jeff's sudden departure. Jeff drove down his street toward Samantha's house. Officer Mullins followed.

Chapter 14

Samantha had really enjoyed her and Jeff's trip to Elephant Rocks. She had thought about the view from the ledge multiple times since leaving. She was sad because she knew that after Jeff got rid of Angus, she would never be able to return.

She had thought about the plan that Jeff had shared with her. When Jeff first uttered the words about murdering Angus, she was shocked. Of course, she had maintained her poker face and continued to listen to Jeff's plan. She didn't dare let Jeff know that she was completely freaked out.

She had agreed to go along with the plan because she was honestly afraid of Jeff McGuire.

At first, Samantha was attracted to Jeff because he owned his own business and was very wealthy. Jeff also provided a means for Samantha to feed her drug addiction. Samantha had quickly developed a strong fear of Jeff McGuire. She had seen him lose his temper over trivial matters.

One time, Jeff had threatened to fight a teenager at a local restaurant. Jeff had asked for extra gravy on his biscuits and gravy platter. The teenager informed Jeff that he would gladly put extra gravy on his platter. However, the extra gravy required an additional charge. Jeff was furious! He told the teenager that they should step outside to resolve the matter. Another manager had attempted to talk to Jeff but he threatened him as well. The police were called and Jeff was removed from the restaurant. All of this because of a 50¢ bowl of gravy that Jeff could more than afford!

Another time, Jeff had caught a pregnant stray cat scrounging in his outside trashcans. Jeff threw a can of soup at the cat and rendered it unconscious. Jeff then took his pocketknife and cut the cat's throat.

Jeff's actions definitely frightened Samantha, but the look in his eyes when he got angry terrified her! The more Samantha saw Jeff's violent temper, the more petrified she became. Samantha wanted to break up with Jeff, but she was afraid he would hurt her, or worse! His plan of murdering his nephew had confirmed her fears about him.

Now that Angus was missing, Samantha couldn't help but wonder if Jeff had altered his plan and had done something else. Perhaps he had decided he didn't want to share his inheritance with her. If that was the case, could she be in danger?

Samantha knew that Jeff had hated his brother. Jeff had told her that he had served twelve years in prison because of his brother and he swore he would get even. When Samantha heard that Jeff's brother had been killed, she was certain that Jeff was involved somehow. But, the newspaper said that Mike McGuire was killed when a 2006 Kenworth Logging truck, driven by Alexander Robertson, failed to stop at a stop sign and collided with McGuire's truck on the driver's side of the vehicle. The report had gone on to say that McGuire had died on the way to the hospital and that his son, Angus, was in critical condition. Regardless of what the newspaper article said, Samantha continued to have her suspicions.

It had taken Samantha a lot of courage. A person that wasn't in her positon would never be able to understand how difficult it was for her. But, Samantha decided that she had to tell the police about Jeff's plan. She had intentionally went to the police station when she knew Jeff was working. She had talked to an Officer Mullins. Officer Mullins had informed Samantha that the police would like her to wear a listening device. Officer Mullins said that if she could get Jeff to admit planning Angus's murder on tape, they could charge him with conspiracy to commit murder. If convicted, Jeff would receive five to ninety-nine years in prison.

Samantha had agreed to wear the wire in exchange for the police's protection until after Jeff was locked up. Samantha had tried on numerous occasions to get Jeff to talk about the murder without being to straight forward. She didn't dare say anything that would make him suspicious. She simply attempted to bring up the subject by mentioning Angus.

One time she had commented on how Angus was always at the house and that they didn't have any privacy anymore. She thought for sure Jeff would comment how she wouldn't have to worry about Angus being around much longer. Jeff didn't. He simply said that he would arrange for Angus to be elsewhere so they could have some fun time. Samantha thought that Jeff was referring to the murder, but she knew without asking Officer Mullins, that this was nowhere near a confession.

Another time, Samantha asked Jeff when they were going to go back to Elephant Rocks. Surely, this would get something incriminating. Nope. Jeff had simply said that they would go back soon, very soon. Again, nowhere near a confession.

After Samantha had made numerous attempts wearing the wire, Officer Mullins had decided that the only way to catch Jeff was to go through with the trip to Elephant Rocks State Park. The police would set up a safety net underneath the rock ledge to catch Angus when Jeff pushed him off. The police would also have hidden cameras set up to film the entire crime so Jeff couldn't claim that it was an accident. It was the perfect set-up. However, now that Angus had possibly been kidnapped, Samantha was very doubtful that she and the police would be able to follow through with the plan.

Jeff had called Samantha fifteen minutes ago and was on his way over to see her. She had to maintain her act of normalcy. She no longer had the listening device from the police. The police had taken it back when they hatched their new plan of catching Jeff in the act. Samantha only knew one way to keep Jeff in a good mood. By now, Jeff repulsed Samantha. But, she had to continue her loving and seductive act. She had put on a pair of tight cotton navy blue gym shorts that were cut to fit high on the thigh and a tight fitting thin white t-shirt.

The doorbell rang. She ran to the door and opened it. Jeff McGuire stood in her doorway as expected. Samantha smiled as if she was genuinely thrilled to see Jeff.

"Come on in Lover!" Samantha said in a flirtatious raspy voice.

When Jeff got through the door, Samantha giggled and jumped onto Jeff and wrapped her legs around his waist. She bit his ear and then attempted to kiss him on the lips. Jeff leaned away and forcefully pried Samantha away from him.

"What's the matter, Sugar Bear?" Samantha said pouting.

"Are you kidding me? Angus is missing. You might as well say four million dollars is missing!" Jeff replied.

Samantha secretly thought about the listening device. If only the police had planted it in her apartment!

"What the hell are we going to do now?" Jeff continued.

"I don't think there is anything we can do baby. You really have no idea where Angus is?" Samantha mistakenly asked.

Jeff didn't answer at first. He seemed to be mulling over the question that Samantha just asked him. He finally responded, "You're thinking that I had something to do with Angus's disappearance? I told you my plan! Don't you trust me? You think I would go behind your back and do something?" Jeff shouted in response.

Samantha's heart began pounding and she felt her pulse in her throat.

"No, baby. I'm not thinking that at all! I just thought maybe you had come up with a better plan and just hadn't had the time to tell me about it yet," Samantha fearfully responded trying to maintain her cool seductive act.

Her poker face was exposed now. Jeff saw through her act for the first time.

"BULLSHIT! You think I double-crossed you. All this "baby" and "lover" crap. That's all just an act. You've been parading and throwing yourself on me in order to get my four million dollars!" Jeff yelled furiously.

Jeff had been under a tremendous amount of stress. He could no longer contain his inner rage. Jeff McGuire snapped!

Samantha was a petite woman. She stood five feet three inches tall and weighed a hundred and twenty pounds. In Jeff McGuire's rage she probably only felt as if she weighed about ten pounds. Jeff picked Samantha up and forcefully slammed her back against the wall. The drywall busted as Samantha slammed into it with a loud thud.

"I'm sorry, baby!" Samantha pleaded as she slid down the wall.

"Oh, you're going to be very sorry!" Jeff screamed as he walked toward Samantha.

Jeff grabbed Samantha by the throat and began strangling her. Samantha tried to speak but her air was completely cut off. Jeff was in a complete stage of fury. Samantha had no doubt that Jeff was going to kill her. She reached out with both hands and dug her thumbs into Jeff's eye sockets as hard as she could. Samantha heard a sickening squishing sound as her thumbs penetrated Jeff's eyeballs and she felt the bone in the back of Jeff's eye sockets.

"AAAAAGGGG YOU BITCH!" Jeff screamed in agony as Samantha continued to dig her thumbs inside his eye sockets.

Surprisingly, Jeff did not let go of his stranglehold on Samantha's neck. In fact, as Samantha dug her thumbs as far into Jeff's skull as she could, Jeff squeezed even harder on Samantha's neck. Samantha was just about to lose consciousness when she gave up on digging out Jeff's eyes and thrust her knee as hard as she could into Jeff's groin.

Despite his rage, Jeff was unable to maintain his hold on Samantha's neck and he let go and collapsed to the floor in pain.

Samantha ran to her phone and dialed 9-1-1.

"St. Francois County 9-1-1 please state your emergency," the dispatcher responded on the other end of the line.

Samantha tried to speak but she wasn't able to catch her breath or speak. In his rage, Jeff had succeeded in crushing Samantha's trachea.

Being blinded and not knowing that Samantha had dialed 9-1-1, Jeff yelled out, "I'M GOING TO KILL YOU!"

The dispatcher sensed the caller was unable to speak and said, "Don't hang up the phone. I have police and E.M.S. in route to your location."

Samantha left the phone off the hook and stumbled out the front door. She was unable to breathe. She collapsed on her front porch.

Jeff, now completely blind, had no idea what was going on around him. He charged wildly through the house swinging roundhouse punches in the air in a desperate attempt to hit Samantha. In his wild flailing, Jeff crashed through Samantha's front bay window. As Jeff went flying through the large window, a large shard of glass penetrated Jeff's neck. Jeff's internal jugular vein was severed. Jeff landed directly on top of

Samantha. Blood from Jeff's lethal wound gushed onto Samantha's thin white t-shirt. Within two minutes, Jeff McGuire was dead.

Officer Steve Pagnozzi arrived on the scene precisely three minutes after Samantha dialed 9-1-1. He saw Jeff McGuire's lifeless body lying on top of Samantha Tillman. It was obvious to Officer Pagnozzi that Jeff was beyond help. He pulled Jeff's body off Samantha and checked her for a pulse. Samantha wasn't breathing, but she did have a faint pulse. Officer Pagnozzi performed rescue breathing on Samantha until E.M.S. arrived.

Samantha was transported to Parkland Hospital. Samantha was intubated and an endotracheal tube was surgically inserted to repair her broken trachea. Samantha also suffered a concussion from Jeff throwing her against the wall. She was expected to make a full recovery.

Chapter 15

On Monday, October 28th 2013, Amber Dunn sat in her living room with her Bulldog, Gus, drinking pumpkin spice flavored coffee. It was Amber's day off, but she was unable to leave her apartment. She couldn't get her mind off the situation with Angus. She had to figure out some way to help Angus. She was certain that somehow, the police were wrong, and Angus had run away to his dad's cave.

Amber turned on the twelve o'clock news hoping to find out that Angus had been found safe. What Amber saw shocked her.

The lead story on the news was about Jeff McGuire's death. The reporter reported that Jeff McGuire died during an altercation with his girlfriend, Samantha Tillman. The reporter went on to add that the police stated that they had reason to believe that Jeff McGuire had planned missing teenager, Angus McGuire's, murder. The police had no evidence that Jeff had succeeded in his plan. The reporter concluded that Jeff's girlfriend, Samantha Tillman, had been seriously injured during the altercation and was being treated at Parkland Hospital in Farmington, Missouri.

Amber couldn't believe what she just saw. Jeff McGuire was dead! Had he killed Angus and hid the body? Amber couldn't bear the thought of that being true.

Should Amber tell the police about her theory of Angus running away to his cave? Amber quickly decided that with Jeff McGuire out of the picture, there was no reason for her not to go to the police. Amber thought about making a simple phone call, but decided she would probably be more convincing telling the police in person. Besides, Amber wanted to be with the police when they went searching for Angus!

Amber quickly showered, put on a pair of Levi's, a St. Louis Cardinal's hoodie, a ball cap, and a pair of tennis shoes and headed out the door of her apartment. The drive to Park Hills took Amber forty-five minutes. The entire drive, Amber thought about the best way to present her case to the police. Amber decided it was best to first explain her relationship with Angus so the police would give her some credibility.

Amber pulled into the Park Hills police station at 1:05 p.m. and walked quickly into the police station.

"I need to speak with Officer Mullins about an urgent matter," Amber informed the officer at the front desk.

"Officer Mullins is in the field right now. Is there something I can help you with?" the desk officer responded.

"With all due respect, sir, I need to speak directly to Officer Mullins. Like I said, the matter is urgent."

"Ok, ma'am. I'll see if Officer Mullins is available. Who shall I tell him needs him?" the desk officer said.

"Just tell him it is in regards to Angus McGuire," Amber informed the officer.

The desk officer announced into his radio, "Park Hills 101 can you 10-19 to base for 10-17 for urgent 10-43 concerning Angus McGuire?"

Amber heard Officer Mullins voice respond on the radio, "I'm 10-76".

The desk officer looked up at Amber and said, "He's on his way ma'am."

Officer Mullins arrived within minutes of the desk officer's radio transmission.

"Good afternoon ma'am. I was informed you have some urgent information about Angus McGuire," Officer Mullins stated as he walked up to Amber and extended his hand.

Amber shook Officer Mullin's hand and proceeded with the speech she had rehearsed on her drive.

"I'm Amber Dunn. I am a nurse at Missouri Baptist Hospital. I took care of Angus while he was at the hospital after his horrific car wreck. Angus and I became very close. Angus told me about his last day with his dad. He and his dad were on their way home from his dad showing

Angus a secret cave. Angus and his dad were planning to spend a whole week at the cave surviving off the land. I don't think Angus was kidnapped. I think he ran away to the cave," Amber said nervously in a single breath.

Officer Mullins scratched his head and said, "With all due respect, ma'am, it's very normal for people that are close to the lost to invent scenarios where the lost are safe. I completely understand you wanting to believe what you are saying. But, we have ample evidence that persuades us to believe that Angus was in fact kidnapped."

At first, Amber was shocked. She had fully anticipated the police listening to her and quickly forming a search team to go find Angus. She hadn't anticipated the officer not giving her theory any consideration.

"What kind of evidence do you have that leads you to that conclusion?" Amber asked the officer beginning to get irritated.

"Ma'am, we had search dogs that tracked Angus's scent to McDonalds. The dogs had a very strong scent of the boy. The scent just suddenly disappeared. That told us that Angus had to have gotten or been thrown into a vehicle with someone. A person's scent doesn't just disappear unless they get in a vehicle," Officer Mullins stated beginning to match Amber's irritability.

"Look officer, I spoke to Angus on the telephone the day before he came up missing. He invited me to go to his cave with him," Amber stated almost begging the officer to consider what she was saying.

"Can't you at least go look for this cave?" Amber continued.

"Ms. Dunn, I appreciate your concern for the boy. I really do. If I thought, your theory was plausible at all, I would check into it. But, it's not. Now, I have other matters to tend to that are of an urgent matter, if you'll excuse me."

Officer Mullins walked back out the front door of the police station. Amber stood watching him in disbelief. Amber thought, *if the police won't find Angus, I will!*

Chapter 16

*E*ven though I had gone to bed the previous night with a belly full of catfish, I awoke famished.

I decided that I was going to attempt the multiple fishing lines from the tree limbs today. I knew that once I had the lines attached to the trees, I would be able to use them multiple times.

I was excited to try the new method I had read about. I grabbed the roll of fishing line, the sinkers, and the hooks. I also grabbed my slingshot. I figured I would practice with my slingshot after I got my fishing lines set.

I crawled out of my cave with high hopes of catching many fish and improving my marksmanship with the slingshot.

First, I needed some bait for my lines. I walked out of my cave, found another tree stump, and started chipping away. I found four large grubs. I was so hungry that I was tempted to eat one of them. But, I resisted the urge and shoved all four in my pocket. My excitement continued to grow as I walked down to the river.

The first limb that I saw was only hanging out over the river about three feet. I attached a sinker, a hook, and one of the grubs to a strand of fishing line. I had to jump to reach the limb and pull it back to me. I held the limb and tied the fishing line to it. I had overestimated how much fishing line I needed for this line, but the current of the river pulled the line perfectly so my bait wouldn't drag the bottom of the river. I did this same method for three more limbs that were hanging out over the water.

Now that I had four fishing lines rigged, I grabbed a handful of rocks and began practicing with my slingshot. I would pick out a leaf hanging on a tree and try to hit it.

I missed about ninety percent of the shots I took, but I noticed that I was quickly improving. I discovered that one thing I was doing wrong was bending my arm. I came to the conclusion that if I held my arm straight after I pulled back the slingshot, I was able to hold the slingshot much more steady and get off a much better shot.

I also found out that I had to take my time and center my target in the very middle of the slingshot. This was probably my biggest mistake during my first outing. I was quickly learning that patience was extremely important!

After practicing for about twenty minutes, I was now able to hit my target roughly every other shot. I was on cloud nine when I realized the significance of this improved skill!

I had been so wrapped up with my slingshot practice that I had forgotten about my fishing lines. My growling stomach reminded me. I looked over to the river and was shocked to see all four of the tree limbs bending down into the water.

In my excitement, I tripped and fell as I sprinted toward the first line. I scraped my knee on the rocks, but I jumped up quickly and continued running toward the line.

I pulled down the sleeve of my sweatshirt to act as a glove. I waded into the river, grabbed the fishing line, and walked backwards toward the bank. I could tell the first fish wasn't very big.

Upon banking the fish, I saw that it was a small sun perch. I placed my boot on its head and removed the hook from its mouth. I used a nearby rock to hit the fish in the head and kill it. I doubted a hawk would steal this fish, but I wasn't taking any chances. I shoved the fish into my coat pocket and ran to the next line.

The next line wasn't as easy as the first. I obviously had a much bigger fish on the line. I again used my sweatshirt as a glove, grabbed the line, and began walking backward. As I began walking backwards, the fish began fiercely pulling on the line. I feared the fish was going to break the line so I let go. I watch as the limb that the line was tied to bent down until it was underwater. The limb stayed under water for several seconds and then I saw it come back up. The limb stayed up momentarily and then the fish again began pulling and it dropped down below the water. The limb was fighting the fish for me! I watched the fight for several minutes. The fish eventually tired itself out and the limb stopped its little dance.

I grabbed the line with my sweatshirt-covered hand and pulled the fish back toward the bank. I was pleased when I saw that it was another catfish. I was even more pleased when I saw that this catfish was even bigger than the previous one. This catfish was close to three feet long! It was the biggest fish I had ever seen caught. I couldn't believe it!

The catfish was way too big to shove in my pocket. I had no choice but to leave the catfish lying on the bank. I ran to retrieve the two remaining fish worried that something might steal my catfish.

The third fish was another sunfish. It was bigger than the first one. By the time I got to the fourth tree limb, there was no fish there. I was glad. I was ready to get back to my catfish before it was stolen!

I was relieved to discover that my catfish was exactly where I had left it. I cleaned the catfish the same way I did the first one and proudly returned home.

I knew I had more meat than I could eat so I decided to try a smoking technique that I had in my survival notebook that was supposed to preserve meat for two to four weeks. In order to do this, I would have to smoke the meat for a couple of days.

I made a teepee style enclosure to set around my fire pit. I used the inner tube that I had found and attached it to the teepee enclosure with pinesap. I attached slabs of catfish meat to sticks and placed them on the walls of the inside of the teepee about three feet above the fire.

I knew the catfish meat wouldn't last me but a few days. But, I wanted to try out the smoking technique. It worked perfectly! I let the catfish smoke for a couple of days and it turned out delicious. It was nice to know that I could prepare and preserve my food. I knew that I needed to start getting some food stored for when severe weather hit. Missouri has some harsh weather during the winter and I had to be prepared. I wanted to be sitting in my cave nice and toasty during the first snowstorm. I definitely didn't want to be sitting in my cave cold and hungry!

While my catfish was smoking, I decided I would attempt to construct a bow and make some arrows. I had instructions along with sketches in my survival notebook.

The first step was selecting the right piece of wood for my bow. My research suggested using hickory, elm, maple, or ash. I found a large elm tree close by. I found a dead stave on the tree that was about six feet long and used my Swiss Army knife to cut it off. The limb was not brittle. It was dead but had not been dead long enough to start rotting. It could still be bent without being too stiff or brittle. I had learned from my research that I could whittle down the thickness of the stave to get the right amount of draw weight so that each end of the stave draws equally. I spent an entire day doing this. It was pretty much a guessing game. I simply wanted the limb to be uniform in diameter throughout.

After constructing the stave to my bow, I created a notch in each end of the bow. I attached parachute cord to one notch and pulled on it until the stave bent to where the cord was approximately ten inches from the center. I tied the cord to the other end. This was not an easy feat, but I accomplished it. After the cord was tied, I pulled back on the cord. A good guess of my bows draw weight would probably be around forty to fifty pounds.

I spent the whole next day constructing arrows. I cut some branches off a nearby maple tree. Because of my research, I chose small branches that were approximately three inches in diameter. I cut off all the nubs from the branches first.

Next, I heated up each branch individually and very gently pushed on the curves in the branches to straighten them out. Of course, this took a lot of patience. If I pushed too hard on the branches, they would crack or break. I made twelve arrows in all.

Next, I began working on arrowheads. I found some small shale-type rocks and used the boulder in front of my cave to shape and sharpen them into a point. I used the parachute cord to attach them to the arrows.

I had a problem coming up with something to use for fletching for the arrows. I had not been able to hit a bird with my slingshot yet. But, I had greatly improved my slingshot skills. I decided that I would go bird hunting first thing the next morning!

・ ・ ・

I woke up the next morning before daybreak. The more tasks I accomplished from my survival notebook, the prouder and more excited I became. I was going to kill a bird today! I would cook the bird for breakfast and use its feathers for fletching for my arrows.

At first light, I began my search for a bird. I decided I would sit for a while in hopes that I would be able to spot a turkey. I knew it was a long shot, but a turkey would be the ideal bird. Not only would it provide me with one heck of a feast, it would also provide me with an abundance of feathers for my arrows.

The first thing that I would need to do was to camouflage myself. I didn't have any fancy camouflage clothes or anything. I had to improvise. I remembered a movie that I had watched with my dad called *First Blood*. It was about a guy named Rambo. In one particular scene, Rambo buried himself inside a wall of mud to hide from the people that were chasing him.

I didn't want to hide in a wall of mud. First, there were no walls of mud in the forest. Second, I didn't want to freeze to death trying to wash all the mud off in the river. I decided my best option was to hide in a pile of leaves. I made a large pile of leaves next to a tree. I sat with my back to the tree and piled all of the leaves on top of me. Now all I had to do was wait and hope a turkey came along.

I was shocked when after sitting for about twenty minutes, I heard a turkey gobble in the distance. I had no idea how to call for a turkey, so I continued to set and wait. Patience is important in a survival situation. The turkey continued to gobble and the sound of the gobble became louder as the turkey got closer to me. I continued to wait patiently. Then, I saw it. Coming through the trees was a large male turkey. I could see that he had long beard that almost touched the ground as he strutted toward me. He had no idea I was there. It was then that I realized that it was going to be extremely difficult for me to draw my slingshot without scaring him away. I knew that as soon as I moved, he would take off.

I let the large tom get within thirty feet of me before I made my move. Luckily, I was downwind or he surely would have smelled me. I already had the rock and slingshot in my hand ready to go. In one swift movement, I lifted the slingshot while drawing it back and fired. I had practiced a lot with my slingshot and I had gotten good with it. But, that shot was most definitely pure luck. As soon as I jumped up, the tom bolted. I swung my arms and fired in a pure millisecond. The rock struck the turkey directly in the head and he immediately dropped to the ground. I sprung up and ran over to the turkey.

I had seen videos where deer and other wild game sprung back to life when a hunter thought it was dead. I was not taking any chances. I pulled out my knife and quickly removed the turkey's head.

That one shot was the single luckiest thing that ever happened to me. Because of that shot, I was able to finish my arrows. Because of my bow and arrow, I was able to eventually shoot and kill my first deer. The deer provided me with enough meat to last almost the entire winter and a nice warm blanket for my bed. I used the bones to make extra fishhooks, arrowheads, and a larger knife.

Chapter 17

After I killed my first deer, I had more time on my hands. I was no longer spending my days constantly scrounging for food to survive. I still occasionally went hunting and came home with a nice fat rabbit, quail, or squirrel for a meal. However, I no longer had to go out every single day to hunt for food. I used this time to refine my tools that I made from the deer.

One day, I was confined to my cave because it was pouring down rain outside. I had a torch made from a pine tree limb lodged in the ground beside me. The sap from a pine tree makes for an excellent torch. I was sitting on the floor of my cave, next to the torch, making a hunting knife. I used deer antlers for the handle of my knife and a large deer bone to create a blade.

As I was sitting there, the ground began shaking. The ground shook for around thirty seconds. The thought of being trapped inside a cave during an earthquake had never crossed my mind. I didn't panic, but the thought of the possibility of my cave coming crashing down on me crossed my mind. I thought about running outside, but just when I was getting up to go outside, the shaking stopped. I wondered if the earthquake had caused any damage to my cave.

I grabbed the pine torch from the ground and walked around my cave to inspect it. I was just about to conclude that my cave was perfectly fine, when I noticed something. I had totally forgotten about the crack in the back wall that I had yelled into on that first day in my cave with my dad. I looked at the crack and it appeared to be bigger.

If not for the earthquake, I may have never decided to try to bust through the crack. I brought large rocks into my cave and used them to hammer away on the crack. The trick was trying to find a rock that wouldn't break.

I went through numerous rocks before I found one that wouldn't break. Even after I found a rock that wouldn't break, it was very hard and tedious work hammering on the crack. I worked all day hammering on the crack and only increased the size of the crack by about an inch. But, after opening the crack an inch and looking inside, I was determined to continue. What I saw was breathtaking. I had to get through the wall!

After hammering on the rock for three days, I had an opening about four inches wide. I was getting really frustrated with my progress. *"This is going to take me a year!"* I thought. I had to come up with a better method of opening the rock.

I sat down and prayed. *"God, please show me the way to open this rock. I am so grateful for everything that you have provided me. I am asking for your guidance in finding a way to break through this wall. I ask this in the name of Jesus Christ, amen."*

After saying my prayer, I decided to take a break from my rock breaking and go hunting. I really enjoyed hunting. I learned that hunting was an excellent stress relief. I was stressed from all of my hard work hammering on the wall and needed a break!

I decided to take my slingshot. I went out into the forest and quickly shot a large rabbit. As I walked back toward my cave and rounded the boulder to enter my cave, I froze in my tracks. My smoking teepee was knocked over. Standing beside the teepee, feasting on the meat I had been smoking, was a large coyote. I should have been frightened, but I was not. I was angry. I was angry that this animal had invaded my territory and was eating the food that I had worked hard to get.

I quickly put a rock in my slingshot and tried to shoot the coyote. He bolted just as I released the slingshot. The rock missed the coyote and flew into my fire pit. I watched as the coyote ran off into the forest.

I was so disgusted. I didn't have a lot of meat in my smoker, so I didn't lose much. It was the mere fact that another creature had invaded my territory. I now understood why animals were so territorial.

I began cleaning up my fire pit. I used a stick to rake the coals of the fire out of the way so I could fix the three rocks that I used to set my coffee mug on to boil my water.

During the coyote's scrounging, he had shoved the teepee across the fire and the rocks were no longer in the triangular fashion that they needed to be. As I pushed the rocks with the stick, I noticed that when I had shot at the coyote, my rock had hit one of the rocks in the fire and broke it in half. I disgustedly removed the broken rock and went to search for another one that was the right size.

It wasn't hard to find a rock of the right size. I placed it in the fire pit and used the coals that I had raked to the side to rebuild my fire. I had to do some minor repair on my smoking teepee. Overall, I probably spent around thirty minutes repairing the damage that the coyote had caused.

I decided to fix my rabbit on my rotisserie. I placed the rabbit on the rotisserie and sat down next to the fire pondering the event that had just occurred.

As I was sitting there, I saw the pieces of the rock that I had once used to set my coffee mug on. The rock had been about two inches thick. There must have been a small crack in the rock that I hadn't noticed. The shot from my slingshot had caused it to break. The more I thought about this, the more it didn't make sense. There is no way I could shoot at a rock and cause it to split in half. Why did this rock do this? Suddenly, I had an epiphany. The heat from the fire must have caused the rock to become brittle. This could be my solution! If I could heat the rock in the crack of my cave, it might be much easier to chip out!

I quickly crawled inside my cave and retrieved the rock that I had been using to chip away at the crack in the wall. I also grabbed the skull from the deer that I had saved and some parachute cord. I crawled out of my cave and ran excitedly to a nearby pine tree.

I used my Swiss Army knife to painstakingly shave the bark off a small section of the tree. Then, I used the saw blade on my knife to saw a V-notch out of the tree where I had removed the bark. I placed the deer skull directly under the V-notch and tied it to the tree using the parachute cord. I saw a tiny dot of pinesap come out of the notch. I knew it was going to take a few days to collect enough pinesap for what I intended to use it for. Therefore, I returned home and feasted on my rabbit.

I spent the next two days resting. The weather was really cooling off, but luckily, the temperature was not below freezing. If it had been, my sap collecting would have been impossible because the sap would have frozen and not drained.

My plan was to smear the pinesap on several pieces of wood, lay the wood inside the crack, and light it on fire. The wood coated in the pinesap would burn for quite some time causing the rock to heat up immensely. When the fire burned out, I would have a short time to hammer away and attempt to break the crack open.

I returned to the pine tree after waiting for three days. I was happy to discover that the deer skull was almost completely full. I gathered several pinecones from the ground and put them inside my coat. I removed the skull and returned home. I placed the skull filled with pinesap high above my fire so it would heat up and thin out. Once it was thin, I crawled inside my cave and used a stick to spread the pinesap onto several pieces of wood.

Next, I placed the pieces of wood inside the crack. Once the crack was filled with wood, I used the pinecones that I had gathered to fill in the holes and put another coating of pinesap in between to hold everything together. I was hoping the pinecones would act as kindling to get the fire started.

I stood back and admired my work. It wasn't pretty, but I thought it was ingenious! I grabbed my torch from the ground, held it up, and lit one of the pinecones. I watched as the pine cones started burning very slowly. That's the thing about pinesap. It burns slowly. Which is why I used it to make a torch.

I continued to watch as the fire spread throughout the crack. The entire center of the crack was now in flames. The fire continued to burn for approximately forty-five minutes. I knew the rock surrounding the crack had to be extremely hot.

I grabbed my hammering rock and started pounding around the crack. Large pieces of rock began falling from the wall. I continued hitting the wall with my hammering rock. Large pieces of rock continued to fall away from the wall.

After swinging like a lunatic for roughly five minutes straight, I leaned into the wall and pushed as hard as I could. The center of the wall began giving away. The broken rock pushed in and fell on the other side. The rock wall turned out to be about three feet thick. I now had an opening about three feet by two feet.

I collapsed to the ground. I was sweating profusely and could barely catch my breath. I laid on the ground until I caught my breath. I thought about my prayer for help. I thought about the coyote and my shot hitting the rock in the fire pit. I smiled when I realized what had happened. I whispered aloud, *"Thank you!"*

I stood back up and looked at the hole in awe. I stuck my torch into the hole and looked inside for the first time. To say I was shocked is an understatement. I was in total disbelief at what I saw. My only regret was that I knew my dad never got to see what I had just discovered.

Chapter 18

*A*mber knew that her conscience wouldn't be clear unless she found Angus's cave. She couldn't believe that the police had refused to at least go look!

Angus had told her how to get to his cave. He had given her very specific directions on how to get there. Looking back to their conversation, Amber thought that it was strange how Angus had been so specific in his directions. It was almost as if fate had brought them to this point.

On November 24th, 2013, Amber Dunn set out to find Angus's cave. She left her apartment at 8 a.m. She drove to Park Hills and out highway O. She followed highway O and turned left onto highway D. She followed highway D for approximately half a mile and turned right when she saw the little church that Angus had described. She continued to follow this road until she saw a large silo on her left. She turned on the gravel road next to the grain silo. She followed this gravel road for about five minutes and she came upon the Indian Tree that Angus said would be there. Right past the Indian tree was the field.

Amber's 2005 Dodge Neon wouldn't be able to drive across the field like Mike McGuire's Ford Bronco did. Amber pulled her car to the side of the road and began walking across the field at approximately 10:15 a.m. The weather was unseasonably warm for November in Missouri. The temperature was 54°. The Sun was shining and there was a gentle breeze in the air.

As Amber was walking across the field, she remembered that Angus had said that it had taken him and his dad about forty-five minutes to reach the cave once they entered the forest. His dad had known where he was going.

Amber began to worry that she could get lost in her search for the cave. Why had she not told anybody where she was going? For a second, she thought about calling her mom and telling her where and what she was doing. Then Amber thought to herself, *"I'll be fine. If I get lost, I have my cellphone."*   Amber had grown up in the country. She was not intimidated by walking through the woods alone.

Upon reaching the forest, Amber made a mental note to periodically break various plants in half to leave herself a trail to follow back out. She hadn't told Angus, but she often watched survival shows on The Science channel. Her favorite was *Survivorman*.

Amber had gone hunting, fishing, and camping with her father when she was a little girl. Amber's father took her on her final fishing trip when she was twelve years old. Amber had been sitting next to her father when he died of a massive heart attack. Amber had held her dying father in her arms. She had no idea how to help him. She watched helplessly as he took is final breath. Amber would never forget the feeling she had as she held her father and cried out, "PLEASE DON'T DIE DADDY!"

Her father's passing was probably the main reason she had become so attached to Angus. She could identify with his grief. Amber had used her father's death as motivation to become a nurse. She vowed to never be in a position where she didn't know how to help someone. She would make it her life's ambition to help people!

Amber walked through the forest looking for the items that Angus had described. She walked slowly, breaking plants and making mental notes of the different structures she passed. After walking for about thirty minutes, she came upon the clubhouse. She knew she was heading in the right direction.

After passing the clubhouse, Amber noticed the smell of smoke. She immediately realized that the smoke could very possibly be coming from a campfire made by Angus. She began yelling.

"ANGUS? ARE YOU OUT THERE? IT'S AMBER. ANGUS?" She listened for a response. None came. She screamed repeatedly but no answer came. She kept walking.

The smoke made it easy for Amber to find Angus's cave. When she saw the trail of smoke in the clear blue sky, she simply kept walking toward it. When she saw the giant boulder by the creek, she couldn't believe it.

She yelled again but again got no answer. A thought suddenly came to her mind. *What if*

Angus had come to the cave and wasn't able to survive. What if she had walked all the way out here just to find Angus dead?

Amber walked up to the boulder and went behind it. Directly behind the boulder was a smoldering fire with some type of teepee contraption sitting beside it. Even though she had watched many survivor shows, she didn't know what the miniature teepee was for.

She saw the small entrance to the cave that Angus had described.

She stuck her head to the cave entrance and yelled, "ANGUS, ARE YOU IN THERE?"

No answer.

Amber's stomach was full of butterflies. Her throat was dry.

"ANGUS?" Amber yelled into the cave again.

There was still no answer.

Amber got down on her butterfly-filled stomach and began crawling into the cave. The whole time she was crawling, her mind was filled with the dreadful image of finding Angus's dead body

After crawling for about ten feet, the cave opened up. The cave was dark and Amber wasn't able to see. Her hands shook as she fumbled with her cellphone to use its flashlight. After what seemed like an eternity, she was able to turn on the flashlight on her cellphone.

As she shined the cellphone flashlight around the cave, she was amazed at what she saw. Close to the door was a bed made from trees and leaves. Even though the bed was somewhat crude in construction, it was clearly a decent bed for a person to sleep on. She couldn't resist. She laid down on the bed. The leaves were surprisingly soft and the bed was very comfortable. She felt the heat radiating from the fire on her as she briefly laid on the bed.

She got up and continued looking around. Beside the bed lay a backpack. She peeked inside the backpack and found several large pieces of smoked deer. She looked to the right of the bed and saw a massive amount of firewood stacked neatly against the wall. The stack ran the entire length of the wall and was about six feet tall.

She walked toward the back of the wall and saw a large hole in the back of the cave. She leaned inside the hole and shined her light inside. She could not believe what she saw!

Chapter 19

*T*here are certain days in my life that are burned in my memory. The day my dad took me to the cave. The day I woke up in the hospital from my coma. The day I faked my kidnapping and ran away to my new home. The day I crawled through the hole in my cave is also one!

I grabbed my torch and climbed through the hole that I had just busted open. Once I got through the hole, I saw that my cave was connected to a gigantic cavern! I couldn't even see to the other side with the light from my torch.

Many years later I would learn that my cavern covered over sixteen acres! The most amazing thing about the cavern wasn't its size. What made it amazing was the fact that a large portion of the cavern was a lake!

I walked around exploring the main portion of the cavern for about an hour. There were large stalactites and stalagmites throughout the cavern. Several of the stalagmites were ideal to be used as chairs. I sat down on several of these numerous time just looking around in awe.

The sound of dripping water was constant in the otherwise silent cavern. I went to the lake, knelt down, and drank the water. Living things cannot survive in lakes inside caverns, so I knew the water was pure and safe to drink. No more boiling water for me!

As I was exploring, I noticed pictures on the walls. I wasn't the first person inside this cavern! There were numerous drawings throughout the main room but the picture that really drew my attention was a picture of two doorways. Inside the picture of one of the doorways was a drawing of a two people upside down. Inside the picture of the other doorway was a drawing of two bird's feet. I later found out that these bird's feet were raven's feet. I had no idea what the drawings meant at the time, but when I found the two doorways that matched the drawing inside the massive cavern, I was pretty freaked out.

I went back to the drawing of the two doorways and looked at them again. I decided that the one drawing of the two upside down people might mean that there is something bad through that door. Why else would the people be upside down? Did one of the doorways lead to a ledge where you could fall into a deep pit? I didn't know, but I was convinced that at least one of the doorways led to something bad. I couldn't figure out the other picture. What could two bird's feet symbolize? I decided that I was not going to enter either of the doors. Not yet anyway.

I was examining some other drawings when I was startled by a woman's voice inside the cave.

"Angus? Is that you?" came the woman's voice.

"Angus? Is that you?" the voice echoed in the cavern.

I recognized the voice immediately. I looked in the direction of the voice and saw a small light shining from across the cavern. I could make out Amber's silhouette holding the light.

"Amber!" I shouted from about a hundred yards away.

"Amber!" my voice echoed.

Amber and I ran as fast as we safely could, dodging small stalagmites that had just begun forming within the past several hundred years, and met in the middle of the cavern.

Amber hugged me tight. I smelled the apple scented shampoo coming from her hair. She was crying.

"Angus, I was afraid you were dead!" Amber said between sobs.

"I'm sorry Amber. I couldn't tell you. I was afraid Uncle Jeff would find out. He's evil, Amber. He is the most evil man I have ever met! I had to escape!" I said as I began crying too.

Amber let go of her embrace, placed her hands on my shoulders, and looked me in the eyes.

"Angus, your uncle is dead," Amber said solemnly.

I couldn't believe the words I had just heard. Maybe I should have been sad. I was not. A deep sense of relief came upon me.

I looked at Amber and said, "What? How?"

"All I know is, he got into a fight with his girlfriend and was killed while fighting with her. There's no reason for you to stay out here, Angus. You can come home," Amber said with tears running down her face.

"Home? This is my home. Look at this place. It's amazing! Why would I want to leave here?" I asked as I looked into Amber's pretty green eyes.

The glowing light from my torch caused her hair to glisten and her eyes to sparkle making her even more beautiful than I remembered.

"Angus, you can come live with me. Besides, my dog Gus would love having you around," Amber said with a smile.

I was completely torn. I absolutely loved my life in the wilderness. My new cavern discovery was beyond amazing. I was still basking in the pure joy of making such a discovery. Now, the girl that I had become so close to, the girl that I absolutely adored, had invited me to come live with her. Please don't get me wrong. Amber was gorgeous both inside and out. But, at thirteen years old, I didn't look at her with hopes of her being my girlfriend. Amber was more like the mom I had never known.

Amber was looking into my eyes waiting for my answer. I finally answered. "Why don't you stay here and live with me?"

Amber's eyebrows went up. She didn't answer right away. I was glad she didn't immediately reject my proposition.

I continued before Amber could say anything. "We will never have to worry about being too hot or too cold inside this amazing cavern. We have a freshwater source right here. I can provide us with plenty of food. I can make more torches to really lighten this place up. We already have plenty of natural furniture to sit on. I will build you a bed. We will have everything that we need right here. We will never have to worry about all of the evil in the world!" I spoke with a great passion.

Amber finally spoke, "Angus, sweetie, I understand where you're coming from. I really do! The world can be a very ugly place. It can also be a beautiful place. I'm a nurse. I worked very hard to become a nurse so I can help people. It's my passion! I want to help you. I can't put into words how amazing this place of yours is. I'm standing right here, and I still can't believe a place like this even exists. But, I can't live here. I'm begging you. Please, come home with me. I promise you that you will be happy."

I was truly touched by Amber's words. I knew she was being sincere.

I looked away from Amber at the magnificent cavern I had just discovered. I had not even had a chance to explore it yet. After looking around at the glorious cavern for several seconds, I looked back at Amber. Amber's pleading eyes was all of the convincing I needed. As hard as it was going to be leaving my new home, I couldn't envision living my life without Amber in it. Now that the danger of Uncle Jeff was gone, I would be ok.

"Ok, I would love to live with you. But you have to promise me that we will come back here to explore this cavern," I said smiling from ear to ear.

"How about this? I will take a week's vacation and we will spend a whole week out here!" Amber replied.

My answer to Amber's question was another long hug.

Chapter 20

I awoke on Christmas morning of 2013 under my warm down blanket. I could smell the aroma of fried bacon and coffee. I rolled out of bed and walked down the hall.

Gus was lying in the hall floor chewing on a bone that was almost as big as he was. He looked up at me and I saw his little nub tail wagging rapidly.

"Good morning, Gus," I said as I patted him on his broad head.

I entered the kitchen and saw Amber pouring pancake batter into an electric skillet. She was wearing black and green flannel pajamas and her favorite bunny house shoes. I walked over to her, wrapped my arms around her, and hugged her tightly.

"Good morning, Mom," I said as I squeezed her tight.

"Merry Christmas, Angus!" Amber replied.

I remembered telling Amber about my dad's famous bacon-stuffed pancakes. I couldn't believe she remembered. That was just one of the many things that made Amber so amazing. She remembered things you told her because she was such a good listener.

Amber and I spent Christmas morning eating bacon-stuffed pancakes, topped with peanut butter and syrup, and drinking coffee; mine with French-vanilla and Amber's with pumpkin spice.

When we were done eating our pancakes, Amber looked at me and said, "Go have a seat on the couch so you can open your presents."

Amber was in the process of adopting me. She had taken me in, and I immediately thought of her as my mom.

I walked over to the couch and sat down. Gus took a break from the massive bone and hopped on the couch beside me.

"I haven't had a lot of time to get you everything that I wanted to, but I did manage to get you a few things," Amber stated with a smile.

Amber set three presents on my lap, walked over to the loveseat, and sat down Indian-style with her phone out ready to take pictures.

I tore into the presents as Amber sat taking pictures. My presents included a survival knife, some fishing gear, and a PlayStation 4. I gave Amber a humongous hug and asked, "Can I hook the PlayStation up on the big screen TV in here?"

"Well, you can. But, you might want to wait until after I give you your final present," Amber said smiling.

"Another present?" I asked curiously.

"Yes, I got you something that I thought you'd really enjoy. But, I couldn't put it under the tree. I have to go next door and get it. I'll be right back," Amber said as she got up from the loveseat, turned, and walked out the door.

What could it be? I thought as I waited for Amber to return. I really couldn't think of anything else that I had asked for, or that I could possibly need. I was so happy. I was about to go to the window and watch for Amber to return when she opened the door.

When I saw what she had, I couldn't contain my emotions. In Amber's arms was the cutest little German Shepard puppy that I had ever seen. I tried to speak, but I was so choked up that I knew if I did, I would just start bawling like a little baby. I kept choking back my tears as Amber walked over and sat the puppy in my arms.

"Angus, meet Zeke," Amber said as I looked down at the puppy.

Zeke wagged his tail profusely and gave my hands a bath. Gus seemed to like Zeke, too. His little bobtail was wagging profusely as he curiously sniffed Zeke.

With tears streaming down my face, I looked up to Amber and managed to choke out the words "thank you".

"There's more that I need to tell you," Amber said as I took my attention off Zeke and looked up at her.

"When I went to your uncle's house to retrieve your belongings, I ran into a gentleman who knew your dad. He informed me that your dad used your dog, MacGyver, as a stud dog. After some searching, I found Zeke. Zeke is MacGyver's son," Amber said with a smile as tears started streaming down her face.

I looked at Amber. I looked back at little Zeke. I was suddenly completely overwhelmed with the deepest sense of joy I had ever felt. I stood up and set Zeke down on the loveseat. I walked over to Amber, gave her another hug, and whispered, "I love you so much, mom!"

Afterword

I hope you enjoyed reading about Angus.

Part 2, *Angus Returns: Amber's discovery* and part 3, *Angus: A New Beginning* are available now on Amazon.com!

Look for part 4, *Angus: Kara's Journey* to be available in the spring of 2018!

Please find and like my author's page, Mark Leon Reeves, on Facebook!

What readers on Amazon are saying about part 2, Angus Returns: Amber's Discovery!

5 STARS! Another excellent story about the adventures of Angus! I didn't think it would be as good as the first, but I couldn't put it down! Some unexpected twists and turns in this one. Definitely will get "nonreaders" hooked!

~ Amazon Customer, Verified Purchase

5 STARS! He made you love the people in the book, I felt like I was right there in the book with them!

~ Tonya Beard, Verified Purchase

5 STARS! A rare sequel that is as good, if not better than the first book. This is a fast-paced book that has no slow spots. An enjoyable quick read for all ages.

~ T.P.

5 STARS! LOVE, LOVE, LOVE! I can see this as a movie. I think there should be a 3rd!

~ Patsy Weddle

5 STARS! Really enjoyed this book. I felt like I was walking along with Angus. Love the scripture as well. I would recommend this book to all. Can't wait to read more by this author and see the movie.

Pam M., Verified Purchase

5 STARS! Amazing books, very hard to put down after you start reading!

Lisa, Verified Purchase

Made in the USA
San Bernardino, CA
18 April 2019